LEVON'S TRADE

A VIGILANTE JUSTICE THRILLER
BOOK 1

CHUCK DIXON

ROUGH
EDGES
PRESS

Levon's Trade
Paperback Edition

Rough Edges Press
An Imprint of Wolfpack Publishing
701 S. Howard Ave. 106-324
Tampa, Florida 33609

roughedgespress.com

This book is a work of fiction. Any references to historical events, real people or real places are used fictitiously. Other names, characters, places and events are products of the author's imagination, and any resemblance to actual events, places or persons, living or dead, is entirely coincidental.

Paperback ISBN 978-1-68549-036-2
eBook ISBN 978-1-68549-026-3

LEVON'S TRADE

1

Gunny Leffertz said:

"There's more than one way to fuck someone over. Do it hard so they never forget or do it quietly so they never know you were there."

The Escalade looked out of place on the construction site. Shiny as a beetle's back. It was parked with the dusty pickups and bangers. The two guys who got out of it didn't belong there either. Black jeans, snakeskin boots, silver rings and print shirts with the cuffs buttoned but tails untucked. One of them wore a Stetson hat, a straw job, had to set him back three hundred dollars. They picked their way over the rutted lot, carefully skirting a pond of muddy water still full from rain two days before.

The rental blocks were going up fast on a hundred-acre lot just off the throughway exit. And they were filling with tenants as fast as they could be built. By the time the first course of block was laid on a thirty-unit the leases were filled out. In a sour economy, constructing temporary housing for uncertain folks was the only bright spot since the Toyota plant had shut down two years earlier.

The pair from the Escalade walked to the men crowded around the lunch wagon waiting on coffee and egg biscuits. They cut out a man standing in line. A few words were exchanged, no heat, no raised voices. The Escalade pair walked the other man away behind Unit Six and out of sight of the others. The laborer walked before the men in the snakeskin boots-just three guys looking for a spot for a private conversation.

Levon watched them from the cab of the company-owned pickup. Its role as a security vehicle was only made plain by the bar of lights bolted down atop the cab. Otherwise, it was just another vehicle in the fleet with the Wiley & Manners Contract Construction logo on the doors. Like the truck, Levon Cade's job was made clear only by the windbreaker he wore over his button-down shirt and jeans. It said SECURITY across the back in big white letters. Other than that, he looked like a site foreman in his Timberline boots and company ball cap.

He was just off a graveyard shift of keeping an eye on the lot. Stacks of block and thousands of board feet could walk off a site like this overnight. A cup of black coffee then he'd clock out and maybe go for a run or hit the gym on the way home.

He sipped the coffee and watched the three men walk away from the lunch wagon toward the corner of the nearest unit. The laborer was known to him or at least familiar. Young guy. He'd been here since the work started six months ago. Dropped off six days a week before sunrise by the jobbers who brought illegals to the site in buses or vans. He was brother or cousin to some of the other men on the crew. Always joking and laughing with each other but all business at hammer time. Guatemalans from their accents.

The trio walked out of Levon's line of sight. He set his coffee in the holder and stepped out of the Silverado to walk around the back of Unit Six himself.

The young guy was on the ground. The hombre in the straw hat was standing with one foot on the fallen man's chest. He leaned on the bent knee to show the prostrate man his teeth.

"You still owe us," Straw Hat said. Guat accent like the man on the ground. They preyed on their own-second oldest story in time.

"We owe you shit," the man on the ground said. He got a silver-tipped boot in the kidneys for that.

"We paid you. Five thousand each. Our families paid," he said, folding up.

Coyotes.

"That was a down payment. You know this word? Now you pay us, every week. Fifty bucks." Straw Hat put more weight on his bent knee. The man under him grunted.

"What if there's no work?" the laborer said.

"There's always work. Pick melons. Suck some dick. I don't care as long as you pay the rent on your ass and I don't have to come around here again."

Straw Hat stood up to step off the man under him, his full weight on the man's ribs. The laborer drew his knees up against the pain.

"Can I help you, gentlemen?"

Straw Hat and his partner turned to see a man, a tall *gabacho,* walking easily toward them from the early morning shadows of the three-story building of bare block and plywood. A rangy-looking white dude in clean work clothes. His eyes were hidden by the shade of the ball cap on his head.

"A private matter," Straw Hat said.

"That's just it, sir. You're on private property. Uninvited." The tall white guy stopped ten feet shy of them and tilted his cap back. Straw Hat could see the scars along the man's brows now. There was hard tissue there, healed from many cuts and breaks. Straw Hat did his share of boxing down in Guat City. He knew the signs of a guy who could take a hit.

"We have business with this boy." Straw Hat smiled.

"That boy's business is working on these units. My business is to see that he does," the white guy said. Professional and polite like a cop. But without the cop's false smile. This guy wasn't smiling or even trying to pretend to.

"Why don't you crawl back up your own ass, *bolillo*?" Straw Hat said in Spanish, teeth flashing and eyes crinkled in amusement. His partner coughed a laugh.

"Does your little mother know you talk like that?" the white guy said back in fluent Spanish. He even used a Guat accent. A twist of the knife.

Straw Hat reached back under the tail of his shirt. His hand stopped, fingers stretched, tips touching the rubberized grip of the handgun tucked in the band there. His eyes were locked on the white guy's right hand.

Somehow a nasty black automatic had materialized in the *gabacho's* fist. One second his hand was empty. The next there was a pistolo in it, its basilisk eye staring unblinking into Straw Hat's heart.

"You two are going to keep your hands where I can see them and turn around," Levon said, closing the gap between them. He jerked his head to the laborer who got off the ground and first walked, then ran back toward the lunch wagon and his tools.

The steel toe of his Timberline driven behind their right knees dropped the two from the Escalade to the dust one after the other. He had the handguns out of their jeans and tossed them aside. Expensive models like their clothes: a Sig Sauer nine and a Kimber in .40. Straw Hat tried to lever himself onto his side. Levon put his boot on the man's skinny ass and turned his leg sharp. Straw Hat let out a sound like a puppy might make and laid his palms flat on the ground again. Levon continued his search, turning up a pair of clasp knives and a hammerless .32 revolver tucked in the partner's boot. The keys to the pimped-out SUV were on a ring with a mini-Maglite. Two packs of Kools. A wad of hard-used fives, tens, and twenties in a rubber band. Another, smaller, of clean fifties in a silver and turquoise clip. A fancy pill case of gold that rattled when he shook it. The Alabama driver's licenses in their wallets told him that they were Daniel Eckenrode of Birmingham and Sean Tobey from Huntsville. Straw Hat and his partner were pictured on the laminated cards. Levon put the wallets in the pocket of his windbreaker and stepped back.

"You can get up now," he said returning to English.

Straw Hat picked up his hat and brushed it off and took his sweet time adjusting it to the right angle on his head. The partner was fussing over a tear in the knee of his black jeans. Levon waited until he had their full attention.

"You boys get in your fancy ride and pull on out of

here. I see you on this site again and it won't end well for either of you."

"You gonna call the police on us?" Straw Hat smiled.

Levon didn't answer directly. He stood looking out over the torn-up ground of the building lot. Some machines stood idle near deep footings dug for units Ten through Fifteen.

"Lot of holes around a place like this. Lot of ground to be leveled," he said and drew down the bill of his ball cap to hide his eyes.

"What about our wallets?" The partner speaking for the first time.

"I didn't see any wallets. Or guns," Levon said and tossed the ring of keys into Straw Hat's hands.

He stood watching the pair walk away. They were out of sight when he picked the handguns up from the dust using a bandana from his pocket.

Levon returned to his truck in time to see the Escalade pull off the site onto the through road in a cloud of yellow dust. The young laborer was already off to his job. The guy at the lunch wagon was lowering the awning, getting ready to head out.

On his way home, Levon stopped at one of those mail service stores with the cute name. He dropped the handguns into a padded pouch along with the wallets, minus the $300 he found inside, and carried the package to the pert little peanut of a girl smiling at him from the counter.

Two days later a deputy at the Perry County Justice Center opened a package machine-addressed to the sheriff. She dumped out three loaded handguns and two wallets onto her desk. Further exploration found the driver's licenses of a Mr. Eckenrode and a Mr. Tobey with the grim faces of two gentlemen of Latino extraction glaring from under the lenticular plastic.

2

Finals were over.

She had no idea how she did. Truth was, she didn't give a rip. They were over and she was free for the next week.

She joined some of her friends for a pub crawl. Girls she met in the first semester at USF and stayed friends with into her freshman year. They started at places near the school and moved south through the night closer to the city. They lost a few girls along the way. One passed out after too many Jell-O shots and was taken back to the dorm by another. Some other girls paired off with some guys they knew. She was down to two gal pals and feeling it, really *feeling* it, when they reached the place called Skip's in North Tampa.

It was at the ass end of a strip mall anchored by a shuttered Winn-Dixie. The only places open were a coin laundry, a check cashing place, and a dollar store. Though they were all dark at this hour. Skip's was dark and cool and the crowd was maybe Hispanic or whatever but certainly foreign. It smelled of stale beer and a tinge of ganja coming from a back room. The music was Euro techno-pump and drowned out the sound from the big screens showing soccer games above the horseshoe bar.

The trio of college girls never had to pay for a drink. Cuervos were being shoved over the bar to them, paid for by persons unknown. She scanned the dark for their benefactors and saw a guy smiling back at her from an upholstered booth. He looked like a cute guy in some vampire show her little sister watched all the time. He was sitting with two other guys who were almost as cute. He nodded to her and she downed her shot before walking over to join him.

Soon it was all best friends forever as her girlfriends matched up with the other two, less cute, guys. They all had accents but dressed well and didn't smell. And they paid for everything with a wave of a hand to the waitress and bartender who seemed to know them. She never saw any cash on the table. These guys were regulars. These guys were players.

It was all fun and adventurous, but free drinks and a few gypsy kisses were as far as she was going to take it tonight. She had a fiancé back in Huntsville and no plans to infringe on the understanding they had. But a little slap and tickle wasn't cheating, right? Just boys and girls, honey. Her panties were staying right where they were tonight. Tomorrow she'd wake up with a banging tequila hangover and a tongue made of gummy felt. Two Advil washed down with a glass of orange juice, a shower, and maybe a nap and she'd be former Miss Sheffield Park High School again. For now, though, it was her night for the good life.

The cute guy was charming and funny. Not as handsy as she expected considering the bar tab he was running up since the girls slid into the booth. Everything was a joke. Even when she asked his name he'd make a joke of it.

"I'm Brad Pitt; you did not recognize me?"

That made her snort. He smiled and told her if he knew she was so unladylike he'd never have asked her over. That sent her into a series of snorts. She slapped a hand over her mouth and roared into the palm of her hand. He was so funny. Everything was funny. Everything made her laugh now until she could hear her own pulse in her ears. It was louder than the drumming beat of the music. It was getting harder and harder to keep her head upright on her neck. She was still fully conscious, maybe a little furry around the edges, but fully aware. A weakness crept over her. She went to stand but her legs wouldn't respond. She braced her palms on the table to raise herself up and they bent under her weight like rubber. She collapsed onto the tabletop.

She felt his breath on her ear. That funny, sexy accent with words meant just for her.

"I know a place. Another place. A better place."

She wanted to laugh but she was too weak now even for that.

3

Gunny Leffertz said:

"Give it time. Losing someone takes its own time. Grief's a stone-cold bitch. You can't win a fight with her. You can't walk away from her. All you can do is move on and get a lead on her, leave her far behind. Only she's always there, following. Over time the bitch mellows and you can let her walk alongside. Give yourself time to get used to the idea that you and those you lose are on the same path and that path only ends when you do."

"I like Wendy's best," said Merry, her mouth full of a double with cheese.

"You do?" said Levon.

"You know why?"

"I don't, honey."

"It's run by a girl. It's the only place run by a girl. McDonald's. Burger King. Carl's. Arby's. All boys."

"Arby is a boy?"

"Sure, he is. Who'd name a girl Arby?"

"What about Dairy Queen?"

"Their burgers suck," Merry said. Case closed—no arguing with the logic of a nine-year-old.

"Well, okay then," Levon said and stabbed some fries into their shared puddle of ketchup.

"Know what we had for dinner last night, Daddy?" Merry said.

"Well, I know it wasn't Dairy Queen burgers."

"Lobster." Merry pulled a face that crinkled her freckled features.

"Maybe I should come and live at your Grandpa's."

"They're like bugs! Big bugs!" she announced.

"Not bad with drawn butter though."

She nodded agreement and took another bite of her cheeseburger.

He drove her home in his ten-year-old Avalanche. She was seated close by him, his arm around her and her head pressed to his side.

"Why doesn't Grandpa like you?" she said, not looking up.

"Oh, he's a daddy like I am and your mommy was his little girl, and he didn't think I was good enough for your mommy," Levon said.

She thought about that for a while.

"Is that how you feel, Daddy?" she said. She shifted to look up at him.

"About what, honey?"

"Will you not like the boy I marry someday?"

"I'll hate him."

"You don't know him." She was smiling broadly now.

"Doesn't matter, honey. I hate him already."

"Even if it's Kristoff?"

Kristoff was a hunky character from a Disney cartoon that Merry was currently obsessed with.

"Especially him. You bring Kristoff around and I'll carve a canoe out of him," Levon said.

He could feel her shivering against him with suppressed giggles.

The doctor had his BMW parked at the foot of the drive so Levon couldn't pull in. Just like every weekend. Levon pulled up to the curb. The doctor, Merry's grandfather and his father-in-law, stood on the porch, eyeballing the truck with distaste. He waited there at the head of the long walk, peering over the top of his glasses, a section of the Sunday paper in his hand.

"You'll come for me next weekend?" Merry said breaking her embrace.

"You know I will," he said. His rough hand gently brushed her hair back in place.

"Can we buy flowers and take them to Mommy?"

"We sure can. Any kind you like."

She rose to her knees and he leaned from the wheel to accept her kiss to his cheek.

"Bye," she said and let herself out of the truck.

He watched her run up the walk to her grandfather. He saw the doctor's last withering glance before they stepped up to the porch and entered the house.

Levon pulled away then and, on his way back to his apartment, stopped by the cemetery at Holy Christ to visit with Merry's mommy.

4

Gunny Leffertz said:

"A mission is honorable so long as your heart and your mind are in the same place and the outcome is just."

"Joe Bob left a message for you to see him when you come in," Candy said from behind her desk in the office shack. That's what they called it, though it was a tidy double-wide decorated like an uptown real estate office.

Levon was clocking in for second shift.

"At the main office?"

"Naw. He's on site today. I'll buzz him." She touched something on her desk and Joe Bob's voice squawked from a speaker.

"Yeah?"

"Levon Cade just showed up, Mr. Wiley," she answered too loud.

"I'll pull around. Tell him to step outside." The speaker went dead.

Levon stood on the roughhewn deck constructed in front of the double wide. The sun was low in the winter sky and there was a sense that work was winding down all over the site. Joe Bob Wiley's jacked-up Dodge truck pulled around from behind the nearly completed Unit Eight. It came to a stop on the gravel before the office shack. Joe Bob waved Levon over and leaned across the seat to shove the passenger side door open. Levon climbed aboard and Joe Bob drove across the site to the through road and toward the highway.

He'd clocked in and was earning, so it didn't matter what the boss was up to. And Joe Bob wasn't talking as he drove. The big man's face was pinched. His eyes were red and tired behind his tinted Ray Bans. The muscles in his neck were tense. Joe Bob Wiley was a local football hero. A high school phenom who went on to more fame at Wake Forest until a wicked hit in his second season ruined his right knee joint beyond any repair that even modern surgery could effect. No limp and only a little pain but no more broken field running for this good old boy. So he came on board Manners Contract Builders as a glad-handing hometown celebrity and found out he liked construction and had a talent for planning. In twenty years, he had his name on the company and was calling all the shots while Winston Manners retired to Florida to fish, golf, and collect a monthly dividend from the growing business.

"You're making what these days?" Joe Bob spoke up as he cruised the center lane south away from the city traffic.

“You pay me fifteen an hour,” Levon said.

“I pay you a hell of a lot more than that,” Joe Bob snorted.

“Well, there’s overtime, sir.”

"Overtime, shit! You're on site more than I am. You clock seventy hours a week sometimes. You earned a four-figure check over Labor Day, son."

"Guys call out. Sometimes we're short, so I come in."

“You got no place else to be?”

“I’m widowed and my little girl lives with my wife’s father.”

“So, nothing but time on your hands, huh?”

“If I’m at work I’m not getting in trouble,” Levon said and watched the endless lights gliding past in the opposite lane.

“You’re ex-military, right?” Joe Bob said and flipped the lever to shift into a right exit lane.

“That’s right.”

“Which branch?”

“I was one of the good guys, sir.”

Joe Bob barked a laugh at that. There was no spirit in it. It was more a reaction of surprise than humor.

They pulled into a place called Andy’s Bunker, nestled in a grove of evergreens between a Home Depot and a Walmart. It looked like it had been there since Prohibition ended. Flat roof and asbestos siding painted in a riot of blue and orange. The sign promised BBQ and ice-cold beer. There were a few pickups on the lot already.

“I need help and I think you’re the man to help me. I’m willing to pay a shitload more than fifteen an hour,” Joe Bob said, turning in his seat. His voice was low. The bullshit and bluster gone now.

"I'm not doing anything illegal, sir," Levon said meeting the big man's gaze.

"And I wouldn't ask you to. Nothing strictly immoral or illegal."

Levon waited.

"I need you to find my daughter," Joe Bob said opening his door and turning to hide from his passenger the sudden well of tears.

5

Gunny Leffertz said:

"Heroes die. I need you to kill. I don't need you to die. I want guys who can die I can pick 'em on any street corner. Heroes. Who needs 'em? Nobody's asking you to look for grenades to jump on. If you do and you live you need to know that I will personally kick your ass until all the shrapnel pops out."

Joe Bob and Levon took a booth at the rear of Andy's Bunker. The place was quiet. The country-pop on the jukebox was turned way down so the four guys at the end of the bar could hear two women arguing on some political panel show.

The bartender brought them a pair of glasses and a pitcher of Coors. Levon didn't touch his glass.

"Go on. Have a beer," Joe Bob said.

"I'm on the clock, sir."

"I'm the damned boss and I say it's okay. And call me Joe Bob."

Levon poured a short beer and took a sip.

"Do you know we've had zero losses at Evergreen Estates? We're close to finishing the first phase and there's not so much as a nail missing from inventory," Joe Bob said.

"That's a good thing, right?"

"And no vandalism. No fights. Nobody showing up high or drunk. Just everything running smooth and easy."

"This is about your daughter?"

"I've never been on a job where there's been zero shrinkage. These Mexes walk off with anything they can carry. Tools. Lumber. Plumbing. Hell, I build it into my estimates. They'll take concrete if they can — wet concrete right out of the truck. And don't get me started on vendors, son. Pirates is what they are."

Levon took another sip, watching Joe Bob drain his second glass.

"The only difference between this job and all those others is you, Cade. I brought you on this summer and thefts stopped like someone turned off a tap. The only variable is you being there near all the time. And even when you're not there, the rest of the security I hired is more on the ball than they used to be and the laborers keep their hands to themselves. You either scare them all shitless, or maybe you've been a good influence."

Levon nodded.

"I looked into you, Cade. I mean, past your bullshit résumé when you applied. I Googled you and you know what I found."

Levon looked at him level across the table.

"I found jack shit. Oh, I found out you were born in Raleigh and when. You graduated high school. You live in a one-bedroom in a complex I built. Your wife passed two years ago and you have a little girl that doesn't live with you and you're in a custody fight with your father-in-law. You have no criminal record and, until a year ago, you were in the service. That sound right to you?"

"That's the public record, sir."

The argument on the television spread to the four men at the bar. They were in a three-to-one deadlock and telling each other how full of shit the other was. Joe Bob waited until the outnumbered party stormed off to the men's room before continuing.

"Only it's not real clear which branch you were in. Your record has more redactions than Obama's college transcripts. You trained with the Navy, the Marines, the Rangers and a few outfits that only had letters and numbers. There's some dates and places but the rest just isn't there. What isn't there tells a story. It tells me you've been places and done things."

Levon let the beer warm in his hand.

"I need someone with your knowledge. I need someone to find my daughter," Joe Bob said.

"I'm not a detective," Levon said.

"Don't you think I hired a detective? A private outfit that came highly recommended. They told me they'd exhausted every lead. Didn't find Jenna. Didn't send my check back either."

"What do the police say?"

"They tell me she ran away. They tell me she's shacked up with some dude. They say there's no evidence of foul play. I know every parent says this but my girl isn't like that. She's serious about her classes.

She's engaged to a nice local boy here in Huntsville. She's not some tramp who'd run off."

"Like I said, sir. I'm not a detective."

"I know that. That's not what I need. I'm figuring you didn't spend your time in uniform repairing air conditioners at Fort Bragg. The story all those blanks in your record tells me is that you were some kind of badass."

Levon took a pull of the flat beer.

Joe Bob removed his tinted glasses and leaned over the table to look into Levon's face. The older man's eyes were rimmed red. His skin was dry as paper. His chin bunched and quivered as he spoke in a whisper.

"I have the reports from the Tampa police and the Hillsborough County sheriff. I have the papers from the agency I hired. Timelines and witnesses and all that. They take Jenna up to a little past midnight on a Friday three weeks ago and they end. I flew down there, I've *lived* there for the past few weeks. And all anyone can tell me is that there's nothing they can do to follow this any further. There's nothing the law can do. You understand me, Cade?"

"You said this was nothing illegal, sir."

"There's the law and then there's *law*, son. I'm talking justice."

"Excuse me, sir, but you don't know what the hell you're talking about."

"I'm talking about my girl. My little girl. You have a daughter."

"I can't say I understand what you're feeling, sir. I can say I'd imagine I'd feel the exact same as you about now."

"But what would you *do* about it?" Joe Bob said, eyes shifting, searching into Levon's.

Levon's eyes remained still pools gleaming from the surrounding scar tissue.

"Fifty thousand. Cash. Tax-free," Joe Bob said in a whisper.

"I'm sorry, sir."

"Please," Joe Bob said. He enclosed his hand around Levon's, pressing it to the smooth glass.

"Drive me on back to the site or fire me, sir," Levon said.

"Why?"

"Because I'm just not in that line of work anymore."

Joe Bob released the other man's hand.

"I'll meet you at the truck. Take you back to the site for your shift," Joe Bob said. He seemed to shrink, to recede into a smaller space than he occupied before.

One of the men at the bar started to make a remark as Levon made his way to the door. Something about two men holding hands and this wasn't that kind of place. He was heading for his punchline until Levon met his gaze for a second in passing. The wag turned back to the bar and drained his Bud instead of finishing his sentence.

Joe Bob dropped him at the office shack. There was no talk on the drive back.

Levon worked his own shift. When Wayne Spinelli called in to say his wife was sick and couldn't watch the kids on her own Levon agreed to work a double and was on the site until morning.

6

Gunny Leffertz said:

"You can't go dying on every hill. There's no honor in it. Custer's famous. For what? For all the times he won? No. For the one time he fucked up. You want to be famous and dead? Your name on a wall? Or do you want to win? You have to know when it's time to back off and when it's time to go grizzly. You have to know when winning the hill is worth the blood and when the hill is just a pile of shit. Sometimes it's not your day to win. Every day is your day to die."

The judge reached for the hockey puck he used for a gavel in place of a hammer. It was autographed by Bobby Orr and encased in Lucite. The judge was a Philadelphia transplant. Each time he brought the puck down he imagined he heard the score buzzer going off at the Spectrum in South Philly.

"I am granting a continuance in this matter until... " The judge held the paper in his hand and lowered his eyes through the bottom portion of his glasses. "February the 12th, 10am in this courtroom. Until then, happy holidays."

The puck came down. He shoots. He adjudicates. The crowd roars.

"Another fucking continuance," Matt Torrance said with some heat once he and Levon were out in the courthouse lobby.

"He didn't even show up," Levon said.

"Your father-in-law? The prick? Why should he show up? He already paid for the continuance. Why waste his own time?" Matt's nose wrinkled in disgust.

"Matt, I know you're my advocate, but you don't need to get this pissed off. It's not like I'm going to pay you extra for giving a shit."

"I need a drink. You need a drink?"

"Coffee. I have a shift later."

They picked a place within an easy walk of the county courthouse. A faux-Irish bar that had been a real Irish bar before the neighborhood gentrified. They snagged a couple of stools at a bar packed with lawyers, clerks, and other cogs in the machine of county politics.

"Is there anything we can do to stop these continuances? This is the third one," Levon said.

"The good doctor is going to continue to drive you into the poorhouse. He's running the clock out on your finances. And, no, there's not a damned thing I can do but stamp my loafers." Matt sighed.

"I'm not getting any closer to custody. Once-a-week

visitation isn't cutting it. Being without Merry is killing me."

"You know if he crushes you on custody, he'll move to curtail visitation or try and limit it further."

Levon nodded over his coffee.

"What did you do to make this guy hate you so much?"

"He blames me for Arlene's death."

"Cancer, right? How's that work? How's he blame you for that? He's a doctor, for Christ's sake."

"I stressed her. I wasn't there. Neglect. I don't know. Grief doesn't have to make sense," Levon said.

"I have to be honest with you; I am not optimistic. At the risk of my own job security, I have to tell you it doesn't look good," Matt said. He swirled a stick in his highball.

Levon sipped coffee.

"Your father-in-law draws a lot of water in this county. He's got money and friends and one hell of a reputation as a neurosurgeon. He's a generations-long local and you're not. Me, I never met a neurosurgeon who wasn't some kind of weirdo, but people actually *like* this prick. Plus, he has the cash to nickel and dime you on legal fees forever. I mean, you're making maybe $30k a year? Less? You'll wind up with nothing and still not be allowed to see your little girl."

"That bad?"

"Worse. Like I said, I feel it. Which means I know it but I can't say how I know it. He's going to win custody and come after you even harder to take away all your parental rights. You live alone in a one-bedroom going paycheck to paycheck. He's not only going to show that you can't support a child but that you shouldn't have access to Mary."

"Merry."

"Say again?"

"Merry, not Mary. Her name is Meredith."

Matt waved that aside.

"Right. Right. Right. What I'm saying is that this doctor won't be happy until you look like the lovechild of Ted Bundy and Tonya Harding."

"Tonya—?"

"Before your time. Generational thing. The important thing is that you have to ask yourself what you want to do now. Do you stop here and be happy with seeing her on Saturdays or go on and have no money and risk never seeing her again until she's eighteen and emancipated?"

"She's nine. That's nine years of Wendy's and hugs in parking lots."

"Right. And you leave her with Gramps and he has nine years to turn her against you. I get it. I've seen this all before. The choice is a shitty one. It's extortion. It sucks." Matt took a gulp of highball.

"What would it take to beat this?" Levon said.

"Money. Enough money to overcome the doc's old-boy influence and bring this to court for a ruling. Enough money to let the other side know you're all in so they stop slow-walking. Do you have the kind of money?" Matt shrugged and took another long pull.

"I know where I can get it," Levon said and walked from the bar, leaving Matt choking on his last swallow.

7

"You said you wanted printouts," Joe Bob said and slid a stack of paper folders across the counter.

Levon riffled through them. Neatly typed reports from an investigation firm in Tampa. Less neatly typed county papers with handwritten notations. There were maps and lists and an envelope packed with an inch-thick stack of bills.

"Expenses. Jabroni money. Whatever you need it for. It doesn't come off the fifty thousand," Joe Bob said.

Joe Bob called it his man cave. It was a daylight basement in his 6,000 square foot house in Liberty Park. There was a home theater and a matched pair of pool tables and a wall of vintage pinball machines. The wall opposite was a gallery of photos, framed jerseys, footballs, and helmets from Joe Bob's storied past. They were sitting at a granite-topped table set by a fully stocked wet bar.

"What do you want for your money?" Levon said.

"Excuse me?" Joe Bob said.

"I need to know what we're talking about here. You

want her found. I get that. What if she can't be found? What if I find her and it's not good news?"

"That's cold talk, son."

"I need the terms. Your terms."

"The money's yours. All of it. No matter what. I need commitment. You're my last play."

"Good news. Bad news. No news. The fifty is mine. That's a lot of trust, sir."

"It's a lot of pressure, is what it is. If you're the man I think you are, Cade. And I know you are. You won't stop until you've earned every dollar."

"Fair enough, sir."

"When can you start, son?"

"If you can cover my shifts this week I'll head down to Tampa tomorrow first thing," Levon said and dropped the sheaf of files into the waiting satchel and the envelope of cash into his jacket pocket.

"Hell, if I can't I'll walk the site myself," Joe Bob said standing.

They shook hands and Levon left the house.

And went on the hunt.

8

Gunny Leffertz said:

"Know the ground. Know it like it's yours. Know it like you know whatever ghetto or dogpatch or holler you came from. Know it like your old lady's ass. Know it till you can walk it in your sleep. Till every blade of grass has a name. Till you own it. Till you know what's going to happen before it happens."

"That was Levon," Marcia Roth said, setting the cordless down on the kitchen table.

"What did he want?" Dr. Jordan Roth said without looking up from his open laptop.

"He said he'll be away this weekend. Something with work. He won't be able to take Merry."

The doctor said nothing. He was reading and scrolling.

"She'll be broken-hearted." Marcia sighed.

"Hm," the doctor said.

"She needs those visits, Jordan."

The doctor looked up at her over the screen. His eyeglasses had dropped over his nose and he was looking at her over the top of them. It was a look she was certain sent interns and surgical nurses away crying. After thirty years of marriage, she was used to it.

"You know it's true. We're her grandparents, but he's her father," she said.

"How many times must we have this conversation, Mar?" He set the laptop, still open, aside.

She shrugged and waved a hand. Dr. Roth sighed.

"Of course she's happy seeing him. He spoils her with junk food and cheap toys. This isn't about what Merry wants. It's about what's right for her. Do you want to see her end up like her mother?"

Marcia turned away from him. He went on.

"And don't tell me he's changed. And so what if he has? One dead-end job after another. He has no skills. No trade. Except for the one the government taught him. We don't even know who he really is. All we know is what Arlene told us and that's not a fraction of what he told *her*. And how much is there that he didn't tell her?"

"So he was a soldier," Marcia said.

"You make it sound like he marched in parades. He was a killer. He killed men for the government. He killed in secret and he must have at least been good at it. He stayed in their service for twelve years. Most of those years he was married to our daughter. Can you imagine the stress she was under? The constant strain of the life he chose?"

"It's over now. He's away from that."

"It's not over for him. That's not something you walk away from."

"He told us, he talked to you, about the PTSD. He was getting treatment, talking to people," she said.

"He was following protocol. Like a soldier. Doing what they told him to do. See a therapist. Take the pills. Stay the course." He snorted.

"Levon is trying."

"You know what I do, Mar. I operate on the brain. That's *my* trade. But you know what the brain is? It's three pounds of greasy fat. But it holds within it the invisible organ of the mind. And no one can know what's in another person's mind. Not really. All I know is that Levon is unstable. Not today. Maybe not ten years from now, he's going to have an episode. He'll return to the feral state, to the wild. I don't want our granddaughter around him when that happens."

She said nothing.

"End of story," he said and pulled the laptop back in front of him.

"You want more coffee?" she said.

"No thank you, Mar. I'm up at six for a procedure. I'll be heading for bed when I finish reading this review," Dr. Roth said and allowed the words on the screen to absorb him once more.

Marcia left the kitchen and made her way back to Merry's room, the room that once belonged to her own daughter. She checked on the girl throughout the night every night just as she had for Merry's mother when she was still a mother herself.

Merry slept in the muted glow of a snowman night-light that Arlene once treasured; it had somehow survived all these years. She was sound asleep in the bed her mother once occupied that was now fitted out with Dora the Explorer sheets and pillowcases. The little girl slept soundly, her arms around a teddy bear wearing a camouflaged army uniform and cap. A gift from her father.

As much as she loved having this little treasure around every day, Marcia Roth wished that all was as it should have been. Her granddaughter asleep in her own room, in her own bed, with her mother and father asleep in the next room.

And as much as Jordan's reasoning made all the sense in the world and was the result of his expert and learned opinion, she couldn't help but think that they were stealing time from their granddaughter. Precious time that should be spent with her own father. And, once again, Marcia felt a pang for Levon who was losing his place in his daughter's childhood just as she had lost seeing her own little girl grow to middle age.

She closed the door of the room, leaving it open only a crack, then went down to the family room where she could read where the light would not disturb the doctor's sleep.

9

Gunny Leffertz said:

"They tell you everyone has a breaking point. Bullshit. There are some men who will die before they break. Those men have something inside. Call it Jesus, bull-headed or what have you. But most men have nothing to cling to. You show that man the empty place in his soul and you've broken him. Fill that empty space with your will and you own him."

The guy was new at Skip's.

Johnny knew most of the regulars, walk-ins from the surrounding neighborhood. There were always fresh asses on the stools and in the booths come nighttime. But Johnny knew this guy was a first-timer.

First off, he was a little older than the usual evening

crowd. Not by much. Or maybe it was the way he carried himself. Most of the nighttime crowd were on their third or fourth adolescence. This guy was more together than that. It was like he was turned inside, keeping to himself. The rest of the crowd was there to be seen. This guy just nursed a draft at the stool farthest from the register.

He was dressed in clean, cool-weather clothes. The weather was turning cold at the start of what passes for winter in Florida. Jeans, a button-down shirt and a light jacket. He was wearing what might have been the first pair of actual work boots Johnny had ever seen in Skip's. The drinkers here were either unemployed, retired, or slumming students from the colleges. Nobody was spending a paycheck.

Maybe a soldier over from MacDill. The guy had that look. But they seldom made it this far off Dale Mabry. And when they did it was always in a group. Same for Canadians, which this guy could be. They traveled in packs. It was the right time of year for snowbirds down from Ottawa and Toronto. Only they were usually older than this guy and came in couples.

Could be a cop or someone looking to hold up the place. In either case, they'd give themselves away pretending not to be looking around. This guy only seemed interested in his beer with an occasional glance up at a football game playing muted on the screen over the bar. He made a single visit to the men's room. Johnny tried to keep track of how long he was gone but there was a rush after ten. The guy was back at the stool gesturing for a fresh draft without Johnny noting his return.

The guy nursed the second beer. He didn't speak to anyone except to nod at a dude asking if he could take the bowl of mixed nuts from where they rested, untouched, by the stranger's elbow. The crowd went from rowdy and dancing to sullen and serious as the tides of beer and cocktails washed over them. The same tide carried them away in twos and threes as closing time approached. The stranger in the work boots wasn't the last to leave but close to it. He left what remained of a twenty for two beers.

Johnny got busy with closing. He counted out the register and put the cash and receipts in a zip bag that he dropped into the slot atop the stout safe set under the bar counter. It was someone else's money. Someone would come and check his count tomorrow. There'd be a crew in tomorrow morning to clean the place. His job was drinks. That's all.

He checked the locks on the front door then shut down all but a few lights until the place dropped into a gloom-tinged orange by the neon Heineken sign in the window. Johnny entered the security code at the back door and stepped into the fenced back court behind Skip's. He worked a row of deadbolts closed in the heavy steel door and turned to his Audi parked alone in one of three spaces.

The guy in the work boots stood by his car. Johnny should have been surprised. He wasn't.

"I had a question," the guy said.

Johnny had a question, too. How the fuck did this mutt make it over the ten-foot fence topped with razor wire that surrounded the back court? The gates were still in place with loops of chromed chain and a big brass lock holding them tight.

"What about, chief?" Johnny's fingers opened and closed. The five-shot snubbie in the waistband at his back grew warm with a heat all its own.

"Three weeks ago, a girl was in here. This is the last place she was seen."

Flat and even. The guy stood easy with his hands at his side. His eyes never left Johnny's. Even when Johnny hit the remote on his key ring making the Audi chirp. The guy never looked away.

"I talked to the police," Johnny said and feinted as if to make for his Audi.

"Now you'll talk to me."

Johnny stepped to drive a shoulder into the guy's gut while reaching for the snubbie with the same move. Johnny was big with a low center of mass. He'd played hockey in a Canadian minor league. In his time, he'd knocked more guys on their ass than a rodeo bull. The old speed was still there in short spurts. His legs drove him toward the guy's unprotected ribs to drive the guy off his work boots.

Only the guy wasn't there.

With nothing to spend his force against except empty air Johnny stumbled. A hand crushed the wrist at his back. His hand never reached the gun. He swung his free hand around to strike, but his fist swept through nothing. An arm snaked around his neck with a rustle of cloth and drew tight.

That's the last thing he could remember.

10

He could hear surf close by. It was cold but he was out of the wind. The floor was steady. He wasn't on a boat.

And, oh yeah, he was buck naked.

Johnny's eyes were covered and he was restrained in a sitting position by what felt like tape. He was seated low on something smooth and cold. His legs were numb. It hurt to flex them. He scraped his toes on the floor, sand on tile. He pressed his foot to the floor and pushed. His seat rocked slightly. He felt ice cold water touch his balls.

The son of a bitch had him taped down on a toilet.

"Anyone hear me?" he called out. His voice echoed back to him from a large empty space. It wasn't a bathroom in a home. It was bigger — a public restroom.

"Hey! Anyone hear me? Is anyone there? I need help!" he called louder.

"I'm the only one here."

The guy. The guy from Skip's. Work boots.

The voice startled Johnny. The bowl under him rocked, sending a splash of chilled water up over his scrotum. The asshole had been there the whole time, watching Johnny sitting stripped naked on the crapper.

"What the fuck, man?" Johnny barked.

"Like I said. I have questions."

"I told you I talked to the cops. I signed a statement. The county sent sheriffs and I talked to them. They sent staties and I talked to them."

"You lied to them, John."

"You know my name. Big fucking deal."

"You lied to them, John."

"What do you want from me? I'm just a working guy making an honest living."

"You're not honest."

The fuck?

"You steal from the owners of that bar."

Johnny said nothing. Was this what it was all about? About his skimming?

"You take home a hundred a night out of the till. Maybe more."

"How do you know, asshole? You see me take from the till? You know you didn't."

"No. You're smarter than that. You keep a new matchbook handy, but you don't smoke. You tear out a match for every five bucks you don't enter on the register. End of the night you have your own count. That goes into your pocket. You went through a whole book tonight."

Johnny broke a sweat. His face was slick with it. It chilled his scalp as the cold air touched it.

"I don't care about that, John. I'm here and you're here about the girl."

"I can tell you what I told the cops," Johnny said after clearing his throat. He fought back the shivers that wracked him.

"You told them lies. I want the truth. You can tell me the truth."

"Fuck you."

"You can tell me the truth, John. You want to tell me the truth."

"Why do I want to do that, asshole?"

"Because whoever told you what lies to tell isn't here. I'm here. You deal with me now. I'm the guy who owns your future."

"You gonna kill me? Is that your big plan, chief?" Johnny tried to gin up some defiance. He was a tough guy. Everybody knew he was a tough guy. Because of that rep, nobody fucked with him. This guy was fucking with him. This guy was all about fucking with people. Johnny's rep was built on the minor league ice. This guy was a major-league goon.

"You know why you're strapped to a toilet, John?"

Johnny held his breath.

"Because I don't like cleaning up after."

Johnny's vision swam even though he was blinded by the tape over his eyes. A gusher of piss exploded from him, creating a fountain sound that bounced off the tiles all around.

"So, you tell me who the girl was with that night. Tell me their names. What car they drove. Anything you know. Anything you can remember. Tell me everything I need to know. And everything you think doesn't matter. Everything. And tell me who told you to lie. Names. Where they're from."

"Then what?" Johnny said with a croak.

"Tell me something good first. Then we see what happens next."

11

Gunny Leffertz said:

"Always be moving. When you're not moving stay hidden. When you're hiding, will yourself to be invisible."

What happened next after Johnny told all he knew was the guy cut the tape holding him down to the bowl. Not even a ripping sound as the blade sliced through the tape holding his wrists behind the pipe that went into the wall. The man leaned close to cut the bands over his legs and gut — no fear of Johnny moving on him. Johnny's arms were locked up with cold and his hands were dead numb.

A sharp snick told him the guy had retracted the blade of a carpet knife back into the handle. Johnny was free to move except for the strip over his eyes. He heard the work boots crunch away over the gritty tile floor. A squeal of rusting hinges. A gust of cold air.

He was alone. The guy was gone. He could hear a car start and pull away, crushing gravel.

Jonny tried to rise off the bowl. His legs felt like they belonged to someone else. They gave under him and he fell against a steel partition wall before crashing to the floor. He lay on the icy tiles and howled as the circulation returned to his hands and legs and ass like liquid fire.

It was a long time before he could make his fingers work to tear the tape off his face. It was gray duct tape. It took off one whole eyebrow. He blinked blood from that eye.

Just as he thought, he was in a public restroom—a long row of stalls with a bank of sinks across from them. The place was familiar. Johnny braced himself on a sink stand and stood up with an effort to look around for his shoes and clothes. The shoes were okay but the clothes were slashed in strips where the guy had cut them off.

Naked and shivering he stepped outside into cold dawn light. He was facing a broad parking lot with trees beyond. Walking further out on the wooden deck he could see the waters of the Gulf. Gentle rollers crept up on a stony beach.

Johnny had been here once before. It was Honeymoon Island, a state park north of Tampa. People would surf cast off the rocks and there was a beach where you could bring your dog. It was closed at night. The guy at the bar knew that. Maybe he was a local. It didn't matter now.

What did matter was for Johnny to get his naked self back to his car and then his apartment in Temple Terrace, grab his stash, pack the car, and get as far as fuck away from Florida as he could before whatever shit the stranger had planned started raining down. This bully knew when to get off the ice.

Those plans struck a hitch when the park rangers found Johnny tramping for the exit wearing only his loafers and a plastic trash bag cinched around his waist to cover his ass.

12

The roof of the derelict Winn-Dixie gave Levon a clear vantage point.

He could see the front and rear of Skip's. Johnny's Audi was still parked in the fenced courtyard from the night before. A van was parked by it now. The van had Eezy Breezy Cleaning printed on a magnetic sign on the side. A fat guy sat sipping convenience store coffee and chain smoking at the wheel.

Around 9:00 am a new BMW purred to the spot next to the Audi. Two men exited. The driver was a stocky guy who wore the last Member's Only jacket on Earth. The passenger was taller and younger and moved with a gym rat swagger. He wore a Bolts jersey with the tail out. The men could have been brothers or father and son. Both had dark wavy hair worn long on top. The older held a leather bag under his arm. It had a clasp atop it like an old-school doctor's bag.

They walked past the smoker in the van without a word or gesture. A flash of gold bracelet when the younger one held the door open for the older. A momentary bulge along the right hip under the jersey. Armed. Both entered and locked the door behind them.

Levon took down the license plate number of the Beemer. He crouched and waited.

Around 10:30 a.m., two middle-aged Latinas exited the back door. Levon could hear the row of deadbolts locking behind them. The pair of women wore matching smocks, jeans, and sneakers. One carried two plastic carry-alls with spray bottles and rags in each hand. The other hauled out a pair of loaded trash bags which she tossed into the rusting dumpster that stood against the back wall. They climbed into the van and it backed out through the fence, piloted by the smoker.

A Rainbow Cab with a sun-faded finish arrived as the van was leaving. It pulled to a stop in the service way behind the strip. A man exited the rear of the taxi. He waved to the driver of the departing cleaning van and entered the courtyard for the rear door of Skip's. The van pulled away with the taxi following.

The newcomer wore a wrinkled polo shirt, baggy jeans, and flip-flops.

Johnny.

Levon picked up his canvas bag and left the hide on the supermarket roof.

13

Gunny Leffertz said:

"You don't get to say it's over until there's no one left but you to say it."

The bar looked like a different place with the lights on and muted sunlight coming through the tinted front windows. Cracks in the linoleum and places where the upholstery was patched with tape. Stains in the ceiling tiles and the overall used, sad appearance of the place swept away the boozy luster that darkness, music, and drinks provided. A sharp stink of cleaning chemicals overrode the smell of stale beer. The bar top was clean. The glasses gleamed in racks. The floor had a dull luster that shrank away as the sheen of mop water dried.

Two men sat in their own Marlboro haze counting and re-counting cash at a booth. They looked up at a rapping sound from the steel door. The younger set down his sheaf of bills and went to the door.

"Who is?" he shouted.

A muffled voice came through the steel and the younger man turned the keys to open the locks and pushed the door open. Johnny entered.

"You on days today?"

"No, Freddy. I lost my keys somewhere. Came to get my spare ring," Johnny said.

"You have rough night?" Fedir said.

"Picked up a blonde. Least she said she was a blonde. I found out different," Johnny said, making his way behind the bar.

"She screw you good?" Fedir grinned, showing a gold incisor.

"Then she screwed me over good. Woke up with my keys and wallet gone down at the Doubletree." Johnny retrieved a ring of keys from a drawer under the bar.

"She rob you, Johnny? For real?" the older man spoke from the booth, hands riffling bills, never losing count.

"Bitch moved like a fucking ninja. Took my cell, too. I never heard a thing, Pat."

Pavlo laughed and waved Johnny over to the booth.

"She quiet in bed too?" Pavlo said.

"Screamed the fucking ceiling down." Johnny shrugged.

Pavlo laughed around the butt in his lips, spraying streams of blue smoke. Fedir took his place in the booth and picked up the count where he left it.

"Now I gotta cancel my cards. Get a new driver's license. It's a pisser. I'll never fucking learn."

"You think with your dick, Johnny. Is okay. Makes you a man," Pavlo said and stripped a few fifties out of the stack he was counting. He held them out to Johnny, who took them with a shaking hand.

"Thanks, Pat. You're doing me a solid," Johnny said.

Pavlo pursed his lips and tilted his head like a dog.

"A good thing. A solid is like a favor. Thanks for the favor, Pat," Johnny said. He was talking too fast. Sweat was standing on his forehead and upper lip despite the ice-cold air pumping down from the ceiling vents.

Pavlo's head tilted at a more acute angle. His eyes grew darker and he studied Johnny's face.

"Nobody move."

None of them heard the guy enter. It was like he appeared in the aisle between the stools and booths like a ghost. A slender guy in a button-down shirt, jeans, and battered work boots. Plastic gloves holding a twelve-gauge with a cut-down barrel. The lethal black tunnel was unmoving and trained on the booth's occupants.

Pavlo turned from the newcomer to Johnny. Johnny raised his hands and shook his head. His eyes said, *I don't know this guy. I'm as surprised as you are.* As a performance, it was unconvincing.

"You rob? You trick us?" Pavlo said to the shotgun man standing in the aisle behind his cousin. His eyes flicked to his cousin Fedir, who was moving his left hand like a slow-motion spider for the automatic snug in the pancake holster on his right hip.

"Johnny. Sweep the cash into the bag," the shotgun man said.

Johnny's head swiveled from Levon to Pavlo to the money and back around.

"I don't want to get blood on it," Levon said.

Pavlo bit through his Marlboro. Fedir's spider hand freeze-framed on its way to the butt of the nine. Johnny jumped to and used an arm to rake the cash into the open bag sitting on the floor. A rubber-banded bundle of twenties missed the opening and slid over the tiles. Johnny stepped away from the booth to reach. Fedir jerked the automatic.

Levon fired through the bench back taking Fedir through the pleather upholstery with a load of buck. He lightning pumped two more loads that punched Pavlo's ribs to splinters and removed his head at the shoulders.

Johnny stumbled, falling back into the stools. Levon chambered a rifled slug and let it fly into Fedir's chest. He plucked the shiny nine-millimeter from the younger man's lifeless fingers. He tossed the empty shotgun to the tabletop. He stepped away and kicked the cash bag clear of the pool of blood spreading from under the booth table.

"You're fucked, asshole. You know who they are?" Johnny said.

"They're who you told me they are." Levon moved the slide back on the nine to see the gleam of brass in the chamber.

"This isn't over. They're gonna send more people," Johnny said.

"That's what I'm counting on," Levon said.

He raised the nine and fired a three-round volley into Johnny center mass. He dropped the pistol to the floor, picked up the bag of cash, and walked out the way he'd come in.

14

Gunny Leffertz said:

"Remember when you were a kid and thought a monster lived in your closet? You'd cry for Mommy and Daddy and they'd turn on the lights and open the closet door. They'd show you the monster wasn't there. Only you knew he was there, didn't you? You knew he couldn't be seen if he didn't want to be seen."

Just before noon cars started pulling up to park in front of Skip's. A few got out of their cars and tried the door. They leaned on the window, shading their eyes with their hands. The tinted glass hid the mysteries inside. Some drove away when they found the place still closed. Others lit up smokes and waited. Noon turned to one and only two diehards were left waiting. They sat on the curb sharing a six-pack of Icehouse one of them picked up at the Shell station at the corner. This was where they drank, damn it.

Creatures of habit. Like barnacles.

Around 1:30 p.m. a four-door Mercedes pulled up to the curb. Two guys got out of the front and shooed the pair of beer drunks away. One held the door and an older guy levered himself out of the backseat. They looked like the two he'd left dead in the booth inside. Except the two young guys had bleached blond hair worn long. They could be twins. They even dressed alike in cotton camp shirts that showed off gym muscles. The man in the rear was older by thirty years or more; his hair shot through with gray.

This guy was upper management.

They unlocked the barred door and entered Skip's. The CLOSED sign stayed in place. Twenty minutes and no change. No cop cars or rescue wagons. A few more customers rolled up and tried the door and walked away. One of the younger guys came out and moved the Benz from the curb to a parking spot and went back inside.

An hour passed and an unmarked van pulled into the fenced-in area at the back of Skip's. Four guys climbed out in work coveralls and removed buckets, mops, and gallon bottles of cleaning fluid from the rear. The group carried all the gear inside. Two came back out to the van. They rolled a pair of plastic fifty-gallon drums from the rear. The drums were empty by the way they moved them. They placed them on a hand truck and wheeled them inside.

They were all white guys.

Levon watched from his place on the Winn-Dixie roof as the afternoon wore on. He had a thermos of coffee in his gear bag and a Cuban sandwich wrapped in paper. He sipped and munched and kept the front and back of the bar under surveillance as the afternoon wore on. He did a rough count of the cash he took. Eighty thousand. Most of it bundled twenties. A lot of money for one night's take for a down-market dive like Skip's.

Cars pulled up and parked and left again as Skip's remained closed. Around 3:00 p.m. a black man pulled up in a Kia pickup and went to the front door. He knocked at the door and waited. The door opened after a minute or so and he was let inside.

The afternoon bartender.

Two more hours and the cleaning crew came out the back. Two of them worked to wheel a drum back to the van. It was heavy now. It took all four of them to lever it up into the back of the van. The rear suspension sagged under the weight. They went back inside for the second drum, also fully loaded. They removed a box of heavy plastic contractor bags from the van. The buckets, mops, and empty cleaning bottles went into these bags. Same with their coveralls, shoe covers, and plastic gloves. The bags were sealed up tight and loaded into the van by the drums. They were in t-shirts and shorts now. Three got in the van and took off. The last one used Johnny's key ring to get into the Audi and drive away.

The black man from the Kia appeared at the front door twenty minutes later. He flipped the sign in the window to OPEN. Like following a whistle only heard by the dogs, the cars pulled up and some of the same folks denied access earlier straggled into the bar.

It was getting on evening when the older man and the twins exited the bar. One of the twins trotted out to the Mercedes. He hit the remote as he moved. The car chirped. Running lights came on. The engine came to life.

Levon shouldered his gear bag and made for the

ladder off the roof. He was in the Avalanche and around to the front of the Winn-Dixie in time to see the Mercedes hooking a left out of the lot to head north. He kept the sedan in sight as he followed across the lot in the same direction. The northern exit off the lot put him out on a surface street. A right turn brought him to a traffic light. He pulled up behind a mini-van and watched the Mercedes cross the intersection ahead of him. The target was almost to the next light by the time Levon was able to make a left to follow. He gunned and weaved and got within three cars of the Mercedes' back bumper. He dropped his speed to match traffic and kept his eyes on the strip of taillights.

The Mercedes took a highway north two exits and got off on a two-lane road lined on either side with run-off ditches and cypress. It was full night now and even darker with the dense marsh woods hemming in all around. Levon hung back and cut his lights. He followed into a subdivision. An elaborate wood-carved sign along the road read Suncoast Estates. The road wound back. Long driveways on either side of the road. Houses sat well back on lots of five acres or more.

Through the boles of the trees, Levon saw the glimmer of the Mercedes' headlights moving off the road where it curved around. Motion lights went on all around silhouetting a sprawling rancher.

He found a dry section of the shoulder and pulled the Avalanche to a stop and cut the motor.

Levon sat a while listening to the ticking of the cooling engine. The headlights vanished into a garage. Lamps went on in the house. The security lights died leaving only dimmer accent lights around the landscap-ing. He punched the dome light override and stepped out of the truck cab. The gear bag held a pair of well-used night vision scopes. He took them along with a long slide .45 pistol. He moved into the woods parallel to the house toward the rear of the property.

15

It was hockey night in the home of Wallace Collins.

Wolodymyr Kolisnyk, formally of Kiev and Lubyanka. Now a year-round resident of Hillsborough County, Florida.

The big screen in the den had the Bolts on. They were playing Chicago. Wally and his nephews would be down in his skybox, but it was an away game. Besides, this was almost as good. The action was crystal clear and the sound system rocked the floor like they were right down there on the ice. And here Wolo had his favorite vodka. Nemiroff Lex. The bar at the Icehouse never had his vodka no matter how many times he told them to stock it for him.

He sipped and watched the game. His nephews bounced on the edge of a sectional, calling out to the players in a mix of Ukrainian and English as if the skaters could hear them. Danny and Van, Danya and Vanko, were twin sons of a man Wolo called brother though they weren't related by blood. Wolo was part of something with stronger ties than any family.

These were bonds forged in the prisons and camps of the old Soviet Union. Parents and siblings and such were mere accidents of birth. That could not compare to the shared suffering offered within the cellblocks and gulag sheds. Wolo's mother gave birth to his body, but the punishment camps gave birth to the man. It was there he earned his place in a brotherhood that welcomed him for his toughness and rewarded him with protection and loyalty. All he had he owed to the men he met there. What did he owe his mother, a whore too stupid to keep a stranger from making her pregnant? She loved her drugs more than she'd ever loved him.

These boys, drinking his beer and spitting popcorn on his carpet in their excitement, were dearer to him than his own son. They were as loyal to him as to their own father.

A commercial came on—some woman showing her tits and talking about pills to make a man's dick hard. Wolo hit the mute.

"What do you think of what happened at Skip's?" he said to the boys.

"A robbery." Danya shrugged.

"Some negros." Vanko nodded.

"They left the shotgun. Why would a robber leave the shotgun?"

"Who knows, uncle? Some negro high on whatever," Danya said.

"And Johnny was not shot with the shotgun. Why is that?"

"They used another gun. There were two of them. There's always two of them," Vanko said.

"How did he get in? Fedir and Pavlo sitting on their asses. Dying like goats."

"Maybe Johnny was with the robbers," Danya said.

"Maybe Oscar too, huh?" Vanko said, brows wrinkled. Oscar was the Haitian afternoon barman at Skip's. He sure fit neatly into Danya's negro theory.

"Could be. Could be. Johnny is not one of us." Wolo sat back and rubbed the gray stubble on his chin.

"We will find them. It's almost $100k. Someone will talk. Someone will notice," Danya said.

"All that cash? You know they will be spending it." Vanko nodded more vigorously.

"Talk to Oscar."

"Tonight, Uncle?" Danya said.

"Tomorrow," Wolo said.

"Game's back on," Vanko said and snaked the remote from the older man's side and snapped the volume back on.

Wolo was up off the cushions and delivered an open hand slap to Vanko's face that sent the younger, larger man tumbling to the floor. Danya barked a laugh. Vanko sat up, a red welt rising angrily on his face. A stream of blood running from his ear.

"We were talking! Business!" Wolo shouted. His hands were fisted.

Vanko lowered his eyes and fought back tears. He was humiliated by the man he called uncle. He was suffering shame at his own show of disrespect. Vanko was pissed at Danya who was sitting with a hand clapped over his mouth to stifle his amusement at the bitchslapping his brother just got in the way of.

Wolo sat back down.

"Talk to Oscar. See what he knows. Watch his eyes. You know how," Wolo said. The final word. His eyes returned to the game.

Vanko was retaking his place on the sectional when the outside lights came on.

16

Gunny Leffertz said:

"You don't want to be seen then act like you belong. Walk like a man and nobody sees you. Scoot around like some half-assed ninja and the shit you call down on yourself is your own damned fault."

One of the bleached blonds stepped onto the screened-in lanai behind the house. He looked this way and that, shrugged and went back into the house through a sliding door.

Levon watched him from well back in the wooded conservation area behind the house. The motion detectors were infrared and well placed. One step from the cover of the trees and ferns and the lights went on all around the house.

The LED spots died after twenty seconds. He raised the NODs scope to his eyes. The property was awash in a greenish glow visible through the lenses. All was in sharp contrast. He moved parallel to the rear of the house and crouched.

The older man and the twins were visible in a family room that opened onto the screened pool area. They were watching TV on a monster screen. They were in for the night. They weren't going anywhere right now.

Levon dropped back into the woods and circled around back toward the Avalanche. Somewhere out in the dark, a coyote yipped into a high howl. They learned to run and hunt at night, away from the eyes of man. Even long-time residents in Florida lived their entire lives and never saw one, though whole packs lived within sight of ex-burb villas and mini-mansions all over the state.

Night was good. Night was a friend.

But some game only came out in the bright of the sun.

Tomorrow was another day.

17

Gunny Leffertz said:

"Not every man has a price. Only all men have something to trade. Most times pride is the last thing on the table."

Levon was back at Suncoast Estates the next morning just after dawn. He parked the Avalanche two properties down from the Kolisnyk house where another monstrosity was under construction. Big place with a crew of Dominicans putting in drywall. His pickup looked right at home on the bare dirt lot. The crew moved sheetrock from the back of the truck into the house without ever looking at him. Another gringo in a pickup. Just one more *jefe* in a work shirt that cost more than a day's wages. As long as he wasn't here to give them shit, they didn't care.

He cut across the back of the property and followed

along the curving road until he came to a clump of low sago palms. From total concealment, he had a clear view of the front of the Kolisnyk home.

A school bus made its way along the road to the cul-de-sac and back. A few cars departed the subdivision for the county road. A landscaper's truck pulled a trailer with a pair of riding mowers behind it.

An old guy shuffled along the verge of the road behind a little white dog on a leash. The dog stopped to sniff in the direction of Levon's hide. The old man muttered something and towed the dog away. On the return leg of their walk, the dog pranced by without turning its head.

The center door of the four-car garage at the Collins' house trundled open. The Mercedes sedan rolled out. The twins were in the front seat. The deeply tinted windows on the sides hid the backseat from view.

They were gone a while when a van pulled up the road and into the driveway. It was marked Eeezy Breezy Cleaning but wasn't the same van as the day before at Skip's. A man got out of the driver's side and slid open the bay door of the van. A woman joined him. Together they carried a tank vacuum cleaner and a plastic tub of cleaning tools to the front door and rang the bell.

Levon moved low and slow to where he could see the front door through the spiky sago fronds. The older man from the day before opened it and held it open for the cleaning couple who entered. He settled back down in his natural hide and drank a bottle of iced tea and ate an egg biscuit sandwich he'd picked up on the way here.

The cleaners were there little more than an hour. They packed the vacuum and attachment back in the van and backed out onto the road. They turned for the exit from the subdivision at the county road. This was their only account in this neighborhood. Levon waited until they were a ways around the curve and walked fast for the front door of the rancher and pressed the doorbell once.

The gray-haired man from the night before swung the door open. He had a second to register shock that it wasn't the cleaners come back for something they'd left behind.

Levon drove a fist into the man's face then stepped inside to catch him as he fell limp. The man was muttering through bloody lips as Levon lowered him to the floor and kicked the door shut at the same time. He drove an elbow to the man's jaw, bouncing his head off the terrazzo tiles. The man stopped muttering and sagged to the floor.

He shot the deadbolts closed and tapped the button on the security system to re-arm it. He took the man under the arms to drag him deeper into the house away from the foyer with its floor-to-ceiling windows of beveled glass. The guy was still toned for his age and heavier than he looked. He was no figurehead boss, this guy. He was muscle once and still a hard man.

Levon had his work cut out for him.

18

His head was pounding as he came around. There was blood in his mouth. A tooth wiggled in a socket. He went to move and couldn't.

Wolodymyr Kolisnyk came around in the sunlight on his own lanai. He was seated upright on one of his own steel lawn chairs. The pad had been torn off. He sat on the bare metal frame. His wrists were duct-taped to the armrests — his ankles to the front legs. There were bands around his chest securing him in an upright position. A strip of tape held his mouth closed. The chair had been moved, so he was out on the pool apron with his back to the water.

A white guy sat on the edge of a chaise in the shade of the overhang. He wore jeans and a work shirt under a cotton hoodie. There were working man's boots on his feet. The man was lean but not skinny. There was scar tissue around his eyes, skin long ago broken and left to heal on its own. The man studied Wolo from under the battle-torn brows.

"I'm going to take the tape off. You're going to speak

in a normal indoor speaking voice. You yell and you go into the pool. Nod if you understand."

Wolo nodded.

"You sure you understand? You let out a yell and I kick you into the water. No one's going to come help you. You'll drown before I'm off your front walk."

Wolo nodded deeper, boring his gaze into the other man's eyes. The man did not blink under his gaze.

The man sat a moment as though making up his mind. Then he stood and tore the tape from Wolo's mouth. The motion brought new pain to the old man's jaw.

"Do you know who I am?" Wolo said low, following the simple rules of quiet the man demanded.

"That's why I'm here."

"Do you know who you fuck with?"

"That's what everybody keeps telling me. If it makes you happy you can tell me who I'm fucking with."

"I am a brother in the Vor. You know the Vor?"

"I do. Some kind of prison gang." The man stood over Wolo, making him look up.

"Is no gang. Is a brotherhood. Is a sacred trust." Wolo spat a stream of blood that missed the leg of the man's jeans by inches.

"I'm not here for that. I'm not here for you. I want to know where your son is."

Dimi? This was about Dimi? What had that little shit done now? Was he the one who robbed Skip's yesterday? Was this a partner of his? Or someone he cheated?

"I do not know where he is."

"I think you do. I think you should tell me right now."

"What is this about? Who is Dimi to you?" Wolo searched the man's face.

"He's someone I need to find. When is the last time you saw him?"

Wolo had no intention of telling this asshole anything, but he could not help but search his mind for the last time he saw his son.

"The girl. This is about the girl — the one at the bar. The one the police were looking for," Wolo said. The skin around the man's eyes tightened just for a second.

"Where is he?"

"All this for some little whore? You come to me in my house. You threaten me. Over a woman? Is this what this is?" Wolo said, a mocking edge in his voice.

"Do you know where she is?"

"In a grave. In the bay. In a whorehouse in Plant City sucking cocks. Do I care?" He shrugged as best he could taped down tight in the chair as he was.

"The last time you saw your son it was about the girl. Was she dead? Was she alive?"

"I cannot remember. I would not help him. He deals in the drugs. The meth. He is no son of mine. He is not Vor," Wolo said.

"You won't help me."

"I cannot help you even if I could. Go see his friends in Cotton Lake. Ask them where he is."

The man put a booted foot on the chair frame between Wolo's knees and shoved. The chair went over backwards into the water. There was no time to call out — no time to take a breath. Wolo's head struck the bottom and lay in the shallow end with his bare feet waggling exposed on the surface. Wolo stared up through water stained with his own blood and willed the man to return with more questions.

The man was gone. He had not stayed. He got what he came for.

19

Gunny Leffertz said:

"Like your boxing coach taught you. Stick and move. Stick and move. Never be where they think you are."

Danny and Van found out two things about Oscar Dumont, the afternoon man at Skip's.

He could take a beating.

And he didn't know anything about the robbery.

Van dropped the plastic sack of lemons he'd been beating Oscar with and told Danny to let the man go.

Oscar sagged away to lean on the bar, a hand to his gut. For sure he'd shit blood for a few days. But he didn't go to his knees.

"You are okay to work today?" Van said.

"I can work," Oscar said turning his face away.

"You one tough motherfucker," Danny said.

Van peeled five $100 bills off his roll and laid them

on the bar. The two of them went out the front to the Mercedes. Van used his throwaway to call Uncle Wolo. No answer. He tried the landline. No answer there either.

"Maybe he is taking a nap," Danny said from the wheel.

Van tapped fingers on the console.

"Forget the pick-ups till later. Let's go have lunch at his house," Van said.

They found their uncle sitting at the bottom of the pool looking up at them like he was surprised to see them.

"This has something to do with the robbery," Danny said.

"You are thinking that? Serious?" Van slapped his brother across the back of the head and wondered, for perhaps the millionth time, how they could have been born seconds apart.

They called the cleaning crew. Then they called their father.

20

Gunny Leffertz said:

"Never underestimate the power of fucking up the other guy's day."

"How's my honey?"

"Daddy!"

"I miss you."

"I miss you, too! Will I see you this weekend?"

"I hope so. I still have some work to do."

"For your boss?"

"For my boss. But I'm going to try and get back. I promise."

"Where are you? Far away?"

"Not too far. Florida. Do you know where Florida is?"

“Where Disneyworld is?”

“That’s right, honey.”

“Are you at Disneyworld, Daddy?”

“Without you?”

“We can go there someday?”

"We will. When I'm done with this work, we'll go to Disneyworld."

“Promise?”

“Promise.”

“Then work hard and come home soon!”

“I will, honey. I just have to see a man and then I’m coming home.”

21

Symon Kharchenko sat chewing a cigar and watching surveillance video on the big screen in the den. His son Danya started to tell him that Uncle Wolo didn't allow smoking in his house. Vanko elbowed him and gave him a sharp look.

Out by the pool, the cleaning crew had Wolo out of the pool and lying on his back on the tiles. Two of them cut the tape from his arms and legs. A third opened a body bag. They'd already brought Symon the contents of his brother's pockets. They lay in a popcorn bowl on a coffee table before the sofa.

The big screen was divided into a grid of six panels like a live action comic book page. In one panel a camera above the front door caught the couple who cleaned the house leaving. This was swiftly followed by the arrival of a man who rang the door then punched Wolo senseless. The man wore a ball cap and the bill hid his face from view. He was white and clean shaven. His clothes were cheap and plain and without distinction. Symon guessed his height at six foot give or take an inch. He was big enough to drop Wolo with a single sucker punch. Wolo, despite his age, was still a very hard man.

The camera over the pool was of no use. It was trained on the pool area but left much of the lanai out of frame. They could clearly see Wolo being slid out to the edge of the pool in the chair, but the stranger was only seen from behind and above. He appeared as shadow silhouetted by the sun glare off the water and only momentarily in the corner of the frame.

Wolo went out well. Though there was no audio, Symon could tell his adopted brother remained stoic and defiant up to the moment where he was tipped back into the water. Symon turned off the image. The sight of Wolo's pathetically wiggling toes above the slopping water was making him sick with rage.

"One white man. You told me you were looking for two negros," Symon said.

"You think this is about what happened at Skip's?" Vanko said.

"Ten years in Tampa and not a drop of blood shed. In two days, we have three of our own dead. You are the smart one. Use your brain," Symon said.

Danya grinned at his brother getting shit on by the old man.

"There is no sound. We do not know what they talked about," Danya said stating the obvious.

"He was talking about Dimi," Symon said.

"How can you tell, *tato*? You read lips?" Danya said.

"I know him well. He made a face he only makes when he talks about his worthless son." Symon flicked a new flame from a gold lighter to bring his Cuban back to life.

"What has Dimi done? Who has he pissed off?" Vanko said.

"Who knows? He deals the drugs. He breaks the code of the Vor and his father's heart and it comes to this," Symon said puffing on the black cigar as thick as his thumb.

"We find who he has made angry then," Vanko said.

"No. You find Dimi and make him tell what he has done and who he has crossed." Symon blew a stream of creamy smoke at the ceiling before standing.

"Then what do we do, *tato*?" Danya said.

"You have him take you to this man. You kill him. Then you kill Dimi. Must everything be explained to you?"

Symon watched the cleaning crew carry the dripping body bag into the house and through the door leading to the garage where their van was parked out of sight. The crew had been busy the last couple of days. The clean-up at Skip's and now the removal of Wolo Kolisnyk.

The pride of the Vor was their invisibility. They ran under cover of legitimate businesses. They paid taxes. Their public face was holding companies that owned fast food places, bars, coin laundries, car dealerships and commercial cleaning companies. These were all used to launder the gains from their true professions of stealing, smuggling and shakedowns. They never wore suits or ties but were the consummate white-collar felons. A criminal conspiracy that has learned to operate in a police state like the Soviet Union easily maintains a low profile in the naïve world of the Americans. The Vor were thieves and extortionists. They never used violence as a tool of their trade. Violence drew attention from the law. The Vor was more comfortable moving unknown and unsuspected through a world of sheep.

Though they could be wolves when needed.

"I want this over quickly. I do not like this risk of

exposure. So far, this stranger has wished to keep his actions hidden from the eyes of the law. He is sending a message meant only for us," Symon said to his sons.

"We'll take care of it, *tato*," Danko said.

"I need your help?" Symon shifted his eyes to his youngest by twenty seconds.

"*Tato*?" Danko said with the voice of a small child.

"I will take care of this. You will drive and you will hold my coat. It is I who will see to the pig who did this to Wolo," Symon said and pointed to the popcorn bowl filled with the detritus from Wolo's pockets.

"Half of what is in the wallet is mine," Symon said and followed the pallbearers to the garage.

22

Levon drove south on I-75 toward Sarasota. He made the exit for Cotton Lake and drove inland on a flat county road. Upscale strip malls and gated communities gave way to dense marsh woods and trailer parks. More and more of the crossroads were unpaved out here. They were just raised sand causeways leading back into wetlands to end at subdivisions or eventually join another county road somewhere.

Cotton Lake turned out to be a crossing of two county roads. There was a gas station attached to a tire store, a no-name convenience store, a combined coin-op laundry and car wash, and a boarded-up two-window soft ice cream place with a roof that was meant to look like a swirl of vanilla but, after years without maintenance more resembled a giant dog turd.

Set back on a gravel drive off the crossroad was a long block building with a steel roof. There were satellite dishes atop the roof and a tall radio mast. Looked like some kind of cracker NASA operated out of here. The metal sign out front, punctuated with bullet and shot holes, said HATTIE'S. There was a steel-roofed portico with rows of picnic benches to one side of the lot. An outdoor barrel-type grill was going hot there and the smell of barbeque was strong. The smoke of it drifted into the slash pines like a fog.

Levon had had his Avalanche lifted and fitted with fat tires after he'd bought it used. But he felt like he was pulling onto the lot in a two-seater MG as every pickup here was raised to the max on tires half as tall as he was. These were swamp runners made to keep moving in mud up to the door panels. Some were beaten to hell and splashed with primer or spray painted in camo. Others looked showroom new with chrome everything and dressed up with name brand accessories.

In addition to the too-tall trucks were a half dozen motorcycles: all Harleys and all custom. One of them had a sidecar with a pit bull sound asleep in the bucket. Levon gave that ride a wide berth. He stepped under the big Confederate battle flag hanging like an awning before the entrance and stepped inside.

The sound system was playing something country from the '70s. Merle Haggard maybe. The interior was dim and cool. There were a few men at the bar at one end of the long hall. The biggest wild hog head Levon had ever seen hung mounted on the wall above the bar. Long ochre tusks and yellow glass eyes that reflected the neon trim lights around the bottle racks.

More men sat at tables spread in no certain order across the open floor. Levon heard a woman laughing but couldn't see her. No one paid any attention to him as he stepped to the bar. The song ended and a new one began—still country but more of a rocking beat. Levon didn't recognize it.

A skinny girl in an aloha shirt worn open over a

bikini top stepped away from where she was talking to two guys in straw hats.

"Help you?" she said neither this way nor that. She could be Hattie. From the age of the sign out front more likely Hattie's granddaughter.

He asked what was on tap. She told him. He ordered a tall Yuengling. She put it in front of him, slid a bowl of boiled peanuts within his reach, and returned to her conversation with the straw hat pair.

Three in the afternoon on a weekday and the place was a quarter full. He walked his beer and peanuts to a table and took a seat. Nobody seemed curious about him. But then they were all still mostly sober.

The music mix shifted from country rock to heavy metal favorites as the sky outside darkened. A big screen in the hall blinked on for a mixed martial arts Pay-Per-View ticket. The pickups departed and more cycles rumbled onto the lot. Levon ordered a second beer and a BBQ sandwich and side of slaw. He took his time finishing that before heading to the men's room in the back. The restrooms were marked BOARS and SOWS.

He was washing up when one of the bikers joined him in the two-sink, two-stall head. The guy was wearing a Jack Daniels t-shirt with the sleeves torn off. It showed off arms covered in tats in a spider web theme. The guy leaned back against the door. No one was coming or going without getting past him first.

"You a jumper?" The guy nodded at the chute and wings inked on Levon's forearm.

"A few times here and there," Levon said. He leaned back on the sink shelf, making no sign that he was eager to leave.

"LALO? HALO? Or just enough to qualify?"

"I've seen the stars in the daytime. Best three minutes of my life."

"Screaming Eagles," the guy said and pulled his collar down to show part of a tat of the eagle head of the 101st Airborne.

"I jumped with them once at Fort Campbell. They mostly stay in the planes these days."

"What brings you to Cotton Lake, brother?" the guy said without brotherly warmth.

"You the official greeter?"

"Nobody comes here unless they mean to. Nobody stays unless they're looking for someone."

"I don't know anyone here."

"And nobody knows you," the guy said.

"You think I'm a cop."

"What am I supposed to think?"

Levon held out his hands. They were big hands with thick wrists and rough with layers of callus.

"Ever see a cop with hands like that?" Levon said. He'd worked two years of construction with Wiley and Manners before moving into security two months prior.

"So, you're not looking for someone. But you're looking for something. Am I wrong?"

"I'm looking to buy."

The guy studied Levon's eyes, searching for some kind of truth in them. He nodded and took his back off the door.

"Give it ten minutes and come on out to the picnic tables," the guy said and left the room.

23

Gunny Leffertz said:

"Folks see what they want to see. Never let them see what you are. Let them see what they want you to be."

The scent of spiced pork still hung in the air even after the barrel grill was shut down for the night. The portico was outside of the lake of white glare a single pole lamp created on Hattie's lot. The only illumination from inside was the glow of a cigarette. Levon took his time walking to the picnic tables, allowing his eyes to adjust to the change in light.

The guy from the men's room sat at a table with another man and a woman. The other man was an older, heavier biker with a dense beard and brittle gray hair held back with a leather-thonged ponytail. The older guy said something and the woman got up and wobbled back to Hattie's, carrying longneck empties.

Levon stood regarding the two men. A scuff of boot soles on gravel behind him. He held his hands out from his side as hands expertly patted him down. They came to the long slide in a pancake holster at the small of his back.

"That stays where it is, hoss," Levon said, eyes on the older man who nodded. The hands left him.

"Sit your ass anywhere," the older man gestured. A patch on his leather vest read DUTCH.

Levon straddled the bench across from the older man, keeping one foot outside. The third man, the pat down man, leaned on a table top off to one side. The guy from the men's room stayed, taking pulls from a Coors longneck.

"Dougie tells me you want to buy. What are you looking for?" Dutch said.

"A half-pound to start. Price depends on quality. If it's good, I'll want a lot more."

"We're talking ice, right?"

"I want anything else I'd be somewhere else."

"How'd you hear about us?"

"Jungle internet. I hear I should go to Cotton Lake if I want to buy weight. My only question is quality," Levon said.

"It's Mexican. You can't get weight domestic. Too many restrictions on the goods," Dutch said.

"That's been our problem. No supply."

"$7k for a half pound."

"$5k. We can up it to twelve for a full bag if the shit is what I'm looking for. I can use five pounds a month to start," Levon said leveling his gaze on Dutch's eyes.

Dutch blinked at that. $60k a month. He smeared his Marlboro out on the scarred tabletop.

"You local?" Dutch said.

"I'm down from up north. Rust belt. Way outside your market."

"You come off 75? There's a Cracker Barrel at the next exit south. Have breakfast there tomorrow."

"That's it?" Levon said.

"That's it. Bring the $5k. Don't worry about the bar tab."

And that was goodbye.

He drove back to 75 and took a room at a Red Roof near the Cracker Barrel.

The next morning the guy from the men's room the night before slid into the booth across from him at Cracker Barrel. He plucked a breakfast link off Levon's plate like they were old pals. Levon gestured to the waitress to fill his friend's coffee cup. The guy wore a print shirt loose. His hair was road whipped.

"You got something for me?"

Levon placed an envelope of bills on the table. The guy took it with a grin for the waitress who loaded up his cup from a carafe. The envelope went under his shirt. The guy took a sip then put a cell phone on the table and slid it to Levon. It was new. A pay-as-you-go burner.

"That's it?" Levon said.

"You'll get a call then you get your stuff. We don't know you."

"But I know where to find you."

"That's right." The guy grinned showing missing teeth. He got up and was gone.

Levon finished his breakfast and paid the check. The cell buzzed as he was walking to his truck. Dutch was on the other end.

"Your goods are under the front seat of your truck."

"This James Bond shit is getting tired."

"We'll get to know each other better. Maybe I'll let you fuck my sister."

"What about the weight we talked about?"

"If you like the shit we can do that."

"When?"

"You keep the phone Dougie gave you. I'll call you tomorrow late. Give you time to confirm how outrageous my shit is."

"Then we do a serious deal."

"We'll talk then."

The phone went dead.

Levon drove north for Tampa. He pulled off at the exit for Seffner and went into the restroom at a Wawa carrying the Target bag he'd found under the front seat of the Avalanche. In the stall, he opened the bag to find a paper envelope containing a sandwich baggie loaded with tiny rocks. They looked like dusty diamonds. He unzipped the bag and dumped the contents in the toilet and flushed.

24

The doublewide sat at the end of Lockhaven Road. A standalone steel garage building with six bays. A primer-shot Dodge Charger sat on the concrete pad by a pair of Harleys. The place had a view of Cotton Lake off the back deck where Dutch Manklin sat counting out the last of the $50.00 bills on a granite-topped table. Dougie sat with him. They were having coffees brought to them by Rachel, Dutch's latest old lady. Dutch poured some flavored creamer into his mug and stirred.

"How can you drink that shit?" Dougie's nose wrinkled at the smell of faux hazelnuts wafting off the other biker's mug.

"You keep up drinking your shit black, you wind up with the reflux, brother," Dutch said while wrapping the stack of Grants with a double strap of rubber band.

"Think this guy's for real?" Dougie said.

"His money is. You told me he went into the Red Roof alone, no reservation. No phone calls. Never talked to anyone."

"We don't know him. This deal could be the set-up. Next time it's him and an army of staties."

"Doesn't matter. We can't handle the weight he's talking about anyway," Dutch said taking a sip of the milky mess in his mug. It left a frosting on his mustache that he licked away.

"It's a lot of money, Dutchie."

"It's a lot of hassle and a lot of heat. Let him deal direct with the Russian. We pick up points off the deal. Ten percent maybe. That's $11k we didn't have last night without any real exposure."

Dutch picked up one of three cell phones he had on the table and punched send then send again. A female voice answered on the other end.

"Tell Dimi to pick up, bitch."

25

The cellphone buzzed and shimmied on the table by the bed waking Levon.

It was Dutch.

"You got a meet two days from now. You know Channelside?"

"Tampa. Where the cruise ships come in."

"That's right, brother. There's a bar. Upper level. The River Rock. Four o'clock."

"I hear you."

"But first you have to prove you're up for the deal. We need to know you're for real."

"How do I do that?"

"Use the cell I gave you. Take a picture of your cash and send it to me. Five minutes."

The line went dead.

Levon got out of bed. Just after midnight. He got the satchel of cash out of the closet of the hotel room. He stripped off the bank bands and dumped it on the bed. He picked up the USA Today still lying where it had been slid under the door that morning. It went on the bed by the cash. He snapped a picture after figuring out the photo function on the phone. Took another for safety then forwarded it to the only number in his send file.

The cell buzzed seconds later.

"The newspaper was a nice touch. You like the James Bond shit after all."

"I have the cash. Do you have my product?"

"We'll talk at Channelside. Bring the cash."

"I'm that stupid," Levon said.

"It's a public place. A cruise ship will be loading and off-loading. There's gonna be assholes off the Carnival Princess everywhere."

"Sunday. Channelside. River Rock. At four."

The line went dead again.

26

Gunny Leffertz said:

"Never let them bind you. Never let them take you to a second place. You won't like it. You fight like a cornered hound or a treed cat. You never, never, never let them take you somewhere else. Even if you have to die. Believe me when I tell, it's better to die on your terms than theirs."

The moored cruise ship towered over the open-air mall at Channelside. The top decks of it were level with condos on the eighth floor of the buildings facing the deep waters of the turning basin.

People in cruise-wear were exiting the ship and complaining that Tampa was colder than they anticipated. Channelside Drive was packed with cars heading for the long-term parking garages. The cruise-bound tourists climbing out of buses and taxis were dressed for Florida winter in layers of sweats. The two crowds, a human estuary of the boarding and debarking, mixed in the mall with idle hours to fill before departure.

The mall was shuttered, a victim of economic downturn and the collapse of Florida tourism. The landed passengers were left wandering empty halls lined with white-washed storefronts. The food court was on the second level surrounded by shuttered theme bars, a locked-up bowling alley, and closed multiplex theater. There were tables and chairs under tattered awnings and tiki-style gazebos. The only food and drink available came from cart services that the city allowed to set up in the empty space.

A stiff wind off the channel sent most of the time-killing tourists off to restaurants within walking distance. Or to the trolley to take them to warm bars and shops in Ybor City ten minutes away. That left most of the tables on the upper level of Channelside empty.

Levon arrived early. He parked the Avalanche on the first level of the parking tower across the street. He joined the growing crowd of new arrivals and drifted up to the food court and took up a vantage point in the shade of an awning. From there he could watch as two men in leather coats took seats in front of the plywood-covered front of River Rock. The rest of the seats and tables bolted down to the deck were empty. They were both young guys with dark hair and carefully trimmed goatees. Both the kind of guys who spend a lot of time on their appearance. Their wrists flashed with jewelry.

At the same time they arrived, three other men took up positions around the food court, doing a poor job of appearing to be casual lookie-loos. They got their coats off the same rack as the seated men.

Each man at the table either spoke on or played with smartphones as they waited. They might have been strangers except that they were dressed like actors auditioning for the same part.

Levon approached using the milling crowd around the hot dog and pretzel wagons as cover. He was right up on the pair before they noticed him. The younger of the two eyed the Nike bag slung under Levon's arm. He took a seat across from them, straddling it with one leg free. The bag went out of sight under the table. The younger man stuck out his hand and smiled.

"They call me Dean," Dimi Kolisnyk said.

"Bill Coates," Levon said.

The other man didn't offer his hand or a smile.

"Cold, yes?" Dimi said hunching his shoulders.

"It's the water," Levon said.

"Still, warmer than Ohio, yes?" Dimi's eyes weren't smiling anymore.

"You ran my plates," Levon said.

"We know you are not called Bill Coates. But it is okay. If your money is good, you call yourself whatever you like." Dimi laughed at his great joke. He was alone in his mirth.

"It's good."

"We see, yes?"

The other man pulled the Nike bag to a place on the ground between them. He unzipped the bag and pulled aside the t-shirt lying atop the stacks of cash bound with rubber bands. Dimi leaned over to run his fingers through the bundles.

"We good?" Levon said.

"Good. Very good."

"Where's my goods?"

Dimi slid a plastic card with a key atop it over the steel tabletop.

"Is in a locker at Gold's Gym. The one off Waters. You can find it?"

"I'll Google it."

"Yes. Google it," Dimi said, amused. "Your stuff is in the locker with this number. The card is a one-day guest pass. Come and go. Stay and work out. Whatever."

"What if I want to reach you again?"

"You use burner that Dutch gave you. He tells me. We set up deal."

"He tell you this is a once-a-month deal?"

"He told me. You like the shit in the locker we do more business."

Levon sat regarding Dimi. The tourists moved past like fish in a pool, colorful and slow. Dimi's lips thinned and eyes narrowed.

"You leave first. Go back to Ohio. Shovel snow," Dimi said, no smile. He waggled his fingers in a shooing motion. The other guy smiled for the first time.

Levon moved away through the crowd for the exit, never looking back. He brushed right by one of the leather-jacketed watchers who eyed Levon all the way down to the street.

He crossed to the parking tower and walked to where the Avalanche was parked. A panel-sided van was parked in the next slot. Levon stopped to turn.

A flash of light turned his world to an explosion in luminescent white before going black.

27

Gunny Leffertz said:

"Body counts don't mean shit if they're not the right bodies."

He'd been tazed before. The trick was to go limp early. Possum up.

His thoughts were coming back together. The muscles in his legs and arms starting to answer to his brain. The burning in the joints was subsiding. The crushing fatigue was still to be overcome.

Fuck that. Fight through it.

Levon was in the back of a van and it was moving at speed. Two figures were trying to turn him on his back, arguing in Ukrainian. He opened his eyes.

Danny and Van. The blond twins. Danny was pulling

Levon's wrists together. He jerked an inch-thick tie-wrap tight around them. Van was crouched at Levon's feet trying to join two tie-wraps to bind his ankles together.

Danny was telling Van that he got his done first. Van was bitching that he couldn't get the two bands to connect.

Levon brought a knee up and drove the heel of a work boot into Van's face. A snap of gristle. A spurt of blood. With the same motion, he brought his joined hands up to drive deep into Danny's crotch. He grabbed a double handful and twisted hard. Danny howled.

Maintaining his death grip on Danny's genitals, Levon rolled, carrying the now shrieking man with him. Danny was atop him, providing cover. Van was backed against the rear doors of the van, rising to his feet. A hand to his nose to staunch the gush of blood running into his mouth and over his chin.

The van came to a violent, slewing halt. Levon and Danny, joined by Levon's grip, went airborne and crashed against the cage mesh separating the rear of the van from the driver's cab. The driver was unbuckling. Levon head-butted Danny in the mouth. He felt the other man's jaw separate with a pop. Danny shrieked in his ear with a gush of fresh blood and broken teeth. Levon relaxed his grip on the man's junk and yanked an automatic from the holster in Danny's belt.

More shouting. The driver and Van. A new weight pressed atop Danny and down on Levon under him. Van was in the fight.

Levon levered the end of the pistol against flesh and pulled the trigger again and again. The weight came off him. Van leaped back crying out, holding both hands to a spreading stain on his thigh. Danny, shuddering, rolled off of Levon leaving him drenched in blood. The van filled with the smell of hot piss.

Lying supine, Levon stabbed the automatic toward the driver's compartment and emptied it through the mesh. A grunt followed by an abbreviated bleat of the van's horn.

Van was trying to get at his own handgun left-handed while maintaining pressure on his thigh. Levon was up and charged across the confining space to shoulder-check the man into the back doors with all his weight. Levon dropped upon the unmoving Van who was going white, bleeding out. Blood pooled in the recesses of the van's floor grid making the surface greasy slick.

Levon yanked a black Sig Sauer from Van's waistband. The man was shivering with the chill that blood loss brings. Levon crawled over him to drop the latch on the back doors and climbed out onto the road.

The van was on the verge of a two-lane with nothing but saw grass and pines visible either side. Levon used the butt of the Sig to break the driver side glass. He reached in over the slumped form of the driver and slid the gear shift to neutral. With a shoulder to the door and a hand holding the wheel to the right, he nudged the van rolling onto the grass. He stepped back and allowed the van to continue down the slope and into a swale filled with black water. It settled in the mud with water up to the windows. The water flooded down through the break Levon made in the glass. The van sank further in an explosion of escaping air until only the top of the roof was visible. Big white birds rose from the surrounding shallows to flap away toward the trees.

Levon was covered in a spray of blood already growing stiff and tacky as it dried. He pulled the buckle from his belt revealing a spade-shaped blade. The razor-sharp edge sliced through the tie wraps on his wrists. He checked his pockets. Wallet and keys were gone. His long slide was probably in the sunken van as well.

There were no rooftops or lights in sight. Only a lonely cell tower a few miles west. He started back up the road the way the van had come. His legs felt like he was dragging sacks of sand behind him. It would take a long hot soak and a long deep sleep to shake off the tazering.

He had a long walk ahead of him before that could happen.

28

Two uniformed Tampa cops found Symon Kharchenko in the communal steam room at his bay view condo complex. He was with a pair of men of his approximate age. All three were covered in tattoos. Prominent on Symon's chest was a snarling tiger. The three men were dressed only in the ropes of gold chains draped about their necks.

The cops stood sweating in their body armor under their starched uniforms. They politely asked if Symon would get dressed and meet them by the pool. Symon twisted his lips and nodded to his *tovariches* before standing and exiting his naked ass out of the hot box.

They weren't arresting him. So it had to be bad news. He showered off, put on a robe and sandals, and joined them in the sunshine by the pool.

The cops told him what they came here to tell him. Symon's granite façade shifted for only a second before regaining his usual impenetrable expression. He thanked the police officers and promised to cooperate with any further questions they may have in the future. The cops left for their patrol car and Symon took the elevator up to his one-level dacha on the eleventh floor.

Once inside, he fell to his knees in the deep pile carpet and wept into his fists while the sun sank over the golden waters visible through the window wall that overlooked the bay. The sky and water were dark and pearls of light along the shoreline were twinkling to life when he lowered his hands from his face. His eyes were red-rimmed and his lips pale. Though damp with his own tears, his expression had regained the density of a sphinx, unreadable and placid.

Only now there was a heat in his eyes, a fire that would consume anything his gaze fell upon.

He would swear to God and Jesus and all the saints that from this day forward his life was divided into two parts. All the days before this day and all the days that would follow. His life with his two boys and his life, from here, without them.

The days left to him would be solely for finding answers. And once he found them, the rest of his life was God's.

But before that, he would get drunk.

Symon made a single call on a cell phone while pouring his first tumbler of Platinka.

"Find Dimi. Tonight."

He tossed the phone to a chair and took a long, burning pull of vodka.

29

Gunny Leffertz said:

"I want my soldiers smart. Courage is good in small doses. Smart is better. A man who's brave all the time isn't smart. He's looking to prove something. A man who's smart knows when to back down, take a loss. A smart man knows it's better to come back another day and win than lose today just to show off his balls."

He was hungry, horny, and sober. Three conditions he found intolerable.

Dmitry Kolisnyk tossed the remote across the room.

Dimi to his family. Dean Collins to his friends.

There was serious shit coming down and his Uncle Symon wanted to talk to him. They dragged him out of a strip club on I-19 in the middle of a private session. All drama, these Old World assholes. Have to make a thing out of what could be accomplished over the phone.

For now, he waited.

He threw himself back in the king-sized bed and looked at himself in the mirrored ceiling. He wore Buccaneers warm-up pants and jacket. His gold crucifix glowed on his spray-tanned chest. He ran a hand over his gym-rat abs — no prison muscle for him.

His father and his 'uncles' were proud of their years inside. They wore getting caught like a soldier wears his medals. Their ink told their story in a kind of illustrated code. Something they should all be ashamed of, and they turned it into a club. Smart criminals didn't get caught. Smart criminals skated. The only ink on Dimi was a Bacardi bat on his right forearm and a winged pixie with big tits on the other. Jesus, he was drunk *that* night.

The red walls of the room were making him crazy. As was the faux gold trim on the heavy Mediterranean furniture and the ankle-deep carpet on the floor. There was nothing on the TV at this hour of the day. Negros arguing in phony courtrooms and white people arguing at tables. He couldn't even look out a window. The black velvet curtains that covered one end of the room hid a bare cinderblock wall.

This place looked like a hotel room, but it was all just a set. It was a property Uncle Symon owned in an industrial park in Largo. He leased it to some Lebanese outfit and they set it up as a porno studio. The Arabs divided it into separate rooms each equipped with HD cameras sending out a live feed of whatever was happening in the rooms. How many couples, threesomes and gang bangs had happened on this bed?

When Symon found out about the operation, he sent his Cossacks to throw the Lebs out on their asses. The Vor was puritanical like that. They'd steal the coins off a dead man's eyes and take the change out of a poor box.

They'd kill and smuggle and extort and defraud without losing a moment's sleep. They ruined lives and bankrupted businesses. But they didn't like dealing drugs and they didn't like whoring out women.

Dimi wondered at that. Most Vor never married. They would keep a woman, sometimes many women, but few stood before a priest or rabbi to take the vows. Their children were all bastards. They owed an allegiance to each other that was deeper than the bonds of marriage or family. Women and kids could come in the way of that; make a man consider choices that were not in the best interest of the brotherhood. Only one loyalty was tolerated. The Vor was all.

One of the many reasons Dimi rejected his father's life. It started as a youthful rebellion. Over time, Dimi saw no value in the company of men who shared a union created in prisons and camps in places so far away. He wanted to be free to do what he wanted; to chase pussy and make money in drugs.

He leapt from the bed and stormed to the room's only door.

"Hey! I am going insane here!" he called to the two men seated at a table in the large open warehouse area outside the row of faux hotel rooms, kitchens, bathrooms and even a phony horse stable with real hay on the floor. The two guys, big guys, were playing cards and watching a live stream of a hockey game from Belgrade.

"Go to sleep. Watch the television," Tupo, a half-Turk said glancing from his hand to the screen.

"Fuck that! The *room* is making me crazy! It smells like shit! There's probably AIDs everywhere from all the faggots fucking each other in there!"

"You want to switch rooms?" Yvan, a Kazakh who looked like Charles Bronson's meaner brother said, laying his hand down to regard Dimi without compassion.

"They are all the same! Dicks and asses and pussies rubbed everywhere! How long do I have to be here?"

"As long as Symon wants you to be," Tupo said.

"Has anyone hurt you? Do you not understand that we are keeping you safe?" Yvan said.

They had not hurt him. They had only dragged him from the club in Clearwater and driven him here the day before. He could not leave. They told him someone was looking for him. That someone killed his father. He was safe for now.

Only Dimi had to ask himself, safe from who?

"Want us to order some pizza?" Tupo said, taking a real interest in the conversation for the first time.

"I don't want any fucking pizza. I just don't want to sit in that jizz-painted room anymore!"

They let him sit with them watching the game — a Serbian team versus Moscow.

That's where he was when the garage doors at one end of the building opened and Uncle Symon's Mercedes pulled in.

His uncle was out of the rear and walking fast over the warehouse floor. Two of his 'brothers' trotted behind to keep up. Symon had Dimi out of the chair and was shaking him. The toes of Dimi's sneakers were squeaking off the polished concrete as he kicked his legs like a man fighting back to the surface of a lake.

"Who is this man? What is this man to you?" Symon said. The tough old bastard dropped Dimi on his ass and stood over him, hands fisted, knuckles bleached white.

"What guy? I don't know who you're talking about!" Dimi shouted in English.

"He knows you. He fucking knows all about you." Symon breathed in and out through his nose.

"What's he done? How's he connected to me?"

"You sold drugs to him? Cheated him? Did something to piss him off enough to come here and start killing people?"

"I take the drugs from the Mexicans then sell them to the guys in Cotton Lake. I don't cheat anyone. I only take my cut. This guy's not Mexican, right? Maybe the bikers know."

"He killed my boys. Did you know that?" Symon said, shrugging his broad shoulders so his jacket lay better.

He did not know that. He did not know anything.

Vanko and Danya.

Now Dimi was scared. Now he no longer felt safe.

30

Merry was surprised to see her dad standing on the front walk of her school.

"How about a ride home, honey?" he said into her hair after she'd leapt into his arms.

A teacher was giving Levon the snake eye and was about to step forward through the crowd of kids rushing for the long row of school buses rumbling at the curb.

"My daddy's home, Ms. Rodriguez!" Merry announced from his arms.

"It's okay if I drive her?" Levon said.

The teacher nodded before being pulled away by a shoving match between two boys arguing over who would get on board the bus first.

Levon and Merry were in the Avalanche heading away.

"What happened to your window?" Merry said.

"Little accident," Levon said. The window at his door was gone. The ride back from Tampa had been a noisy one.

"Did you get hurt?"

"Nothing seeing you didn't cure."

"Was it your fault?"

"What if I told you it was? What if I told you that Daddy forgot his car keys and busted out the window himself?"

Merry laughed.

"Didn't know you had a daddy that dumb, huh?"

She rocked forward against her seat belt giggling.

"Better hope you take after Mommy, huh?"

She slapped his arm to make him stop.

"You're taking me to Grandpa and Grandma's? Because this isn't the way," she said when she'd recovered.

"Honey. How much do you trust your Daddy?" he said, eyes on the road.

"About what?"

"About everything. How much do you trust me?"

"What do you mean?"

"I mean, do you believe me? When I tell you something, you know you can believe me, right?"

"You're my Daddy. You'd never lie to me."

Levon looked at her sitting by him, regarding him with searching eyes.

"Look, Daddy made a mistake. And now I have to fix it," he said.

"Like the window?" Merry said.

"Something like that. For now, I can't have you staying with your grandparents. I need you to come with me."

"Where to?"

"To some friends of mine. Very old friends that are like family to me. They'll be family to you, too."

"What about school?" she said.

"You have your books?" he said.

She patted the book bag on the seat between them.

"Then trust me, honey. You're going to learn a whole lot more than they could ever teach you in school."

He pulled up a ramp onto Lee Highway west. They passed under a state highway sign that read MISSISSIPPI.

31

Gunny Leffertz said:

"Sometimes you go it alone. Sometimes, for the good of all, you break contact and continue the mission."

Symon's lawyer, a smart Jew with political ambitions, secured a copy of the Tampa police file on the sunken van. The evidence found with the three bodies within was detailed in the report. It was worth the thousand dollars Symon paid for it even if the Jew kept half the bribe intended for the evidence clerk at the police center. "Billable hours" was a lawyer word for theft. Symon, an old thief himself, could respect that.

The three men all suffered gunshot wounds at close range. Two of the dead, Danya Kharchenko and Vasily

Gorky, died of gunshot wounds. Vanko Kharchenko was awaiting further autopsy, but notes suggested he may have died of drowning.

The firearms suspected of causing the fatal wounds as well as a potentially mortal wound to V. Kharchenko's thigh were both found within the van. Found as well was a handgun registered to V. Gorky in the state of Florida. In addition was a custom-made .45 automatic in stainless finish. The automatic was equipped with an aftermarket slide tooled without a serial number. Numbers were also absent from the parts on the rest of the weapon.

The nature of the crime scene had a negative effect on the accuracy of any forensic evidence. The van was five or more hours in muddy water before being discovered by a carload of German tourists who stopped to pee in the grass along the run-off swale. Time of death was going to be approximate. Even the hoary old crime-busting cliché of the stopped watch was thwarted by each of the three dead men wearing very high-end and very waterproof watches.

Two solid bits of evidence were unaffected by being submersed in the brackish swill. A man's wallet containing over a thousand dollars in cash, a Shell card, and a driver's license and registration from Alabama. There was also a key ring with a remote for a Chevy vehicle. That matched the registration paper. A ten-year-old Avalanche.

The photocopy of the license showed a white man in close-cropped hair looking dead-eyed into the camera.

"Could be the man I saw on the video at Wolo's," Symon said to the gathering of men in the living room of his condo. The room was dense with smoke from cigars and cigarettes.

They were young and old. Ukrainians, Russians, Armenians, and Latvians. All were Vor. All cooperated in a blood brotherhood that went beyond race or language or family, with rules and a code of honor more rigid than any army. They called themselves "thieves-in-law" and answered only to their own set of laws and recognized no other.

"What is his business with us?" said an Armenian named Yuri.

"He is nothing to us. He has dealings with Dimi, Wolo's son," Symon said.

One of the men made a spitting sound at the mention of Dimi's name.

"Danya and Vanko were looking for Dimi. They must have found the man from the video. Tried to take him captive. Something went wrong," Symon said.

"The robbery at Skip's. Wolo dead. Your sons dead. This is not only about that piece of shit Dimi," said Oreske, a man older than Symon and underboss to the Vor chief in Miami.

"Dimi sold the man drugs. The man paid him with money I believe came from the robbery at Skip's," Symon said.

"Who told you this?" Oreske said.

"Dimi. I have him. He told me what he knows. Or as much as he wants me to know. He says he never met the man. Dimi does not know him except through some gang Dimi has business with," Symon said.

"He must know. Dimi must know what this man is about, why he is in Tampa making hell for us," Soshi, a fat Georgian, said.

"Dimi knows he is the key to all of this. He knows that as long as we have questions, I will allow him to live. I say we ask the man himself," Symon said and held up an enlarged photocopy of the driver's license of Levon Edward Cade of 1001 Willow Run Rd, apartment 3A, Moore's Mill, Alabama.

32

Gunny Leffertz said:

"You can't always choose your enemies. Some days they choose you."

Joe Bob Wiley's cell twanged two bars of "I Walk the Line." He plucked it off his belt—unknown number.

"You got Joe Bob. What can I do for you?"

"Mr. Wiley. Don't say my name."

"Hell, son. I thought you ran off on me. What have you learned? Can you tell me anything?"

"I'm getting closer, sir. There's been a snag."

"What about Jenna? You find out something?"

"It's pretty involved. I know all the players now."

"That doesn't help my wife or me. I need you to do what I'm paying you for."

"I understand that, sir. I just don't have anything for you right now."

"Well, pardon my asking but why the hell'd you call me then?"

"The players I talked about, sir. They know who I am now."

"Shit."

"That's all on me, sir. I'm dealing with it now."

"You telling me that if they know you then they know me."

"No, sir. There's no connection between me and you and why I'm here."

"Then what do you want me to do?"

"Just an FYI, sir. Keeping you informed."

"Just find Jenna."

"I will, sir. You have my word."

The line went dead.

Less than an hour passed and the reception desk called.

"Outside call for you, Mr. Wiley. Line four."

"Who is it, Debbie?"

"She says she's from Gulfside Moving and Storage. Question about an employee."

He punched line four.

"You got Joe Bob. What can I do for you?"

"This is human resources for Gulfside Moving. Is this someone in charge?"

"Only the goddamned owner, honey. Joseph Wiley of Wiley-Manners."

"We wanted to talk to your Human Resources department but we're told you don't have one." The woman on the other end had an edge of nervousness to it. It sounded like her first day on the job. Or she was lying.

"I do all the hiring here. Where you calling from?"

A pause.

Another voice behind her.

"We're in the Tampa Bay area. I'm calling based on a reference on an employment application to be a driver for us."

"Who's applying?"

"Levon Edward Cade. He works for you in some capacity?"

Joe Bob covered the phone and took a deep breath.

"That son of a bitch? I fired his ass a month ago. You mean that dumb bastard had the balls to put me down as a work reference? That boy's dumber than shit, I tell you. That's why I fired his ass."

Another pause. The rasp of a hand covering the phone on the other end. Muffled voices.

"Hello? You still there?" Joe Bob said.

"And do you know his current location, Mr. Wiley?"

"Why the hell would I know that? Shithead could fall off the planet for all I care. All's I'm saying is he's not worth the hire. You hearing me, honey?"

"Thank you for your assistance. Have a nice day."

The line went dead.

Joe Bob sat back in his chair. The back of his shirt was soaked with sweat. His throat felt dry as paper. He pulled a bottom drawer out of his desk and retrieved a bottle of Maker's Mark that had been unopened since a vendor gifted it to him last Christmas. He poured a long slug to top off his lukewarm mug of coffee.

What the hell did you get yourself into, Levon? And what the hell did you get me *into?*

33

The two men sat side by side in first class on the short leg flight to Huntsville. Their leather coats creaked but they declined the attendant's offer to put them in the overhead.

Karp was a big man. He struggled to find a comfortable position even in the wider premium seat. His right arm took up the entire console arm between himself and his traveling partner.

Nestor shrugged against the window, fiddling with a tablet. His fingers sliding across the screen pecking and swiping. He was slighter than Karp with a boy's face that made him almost as pretty as a girl if not for a predator look apparent in his ice-grey eyes. His shoulder-length chestnut hair was worn loose to hide those eyes from those he hunted until it was too late.

They were airborne from Tampa with vodkas between them. Nestor took his with ice. He'd become an American. Karp found that contemptuous, but they no longer spoke of it.

"This Levon. It is as if he did not exist," Nestor said in Russian, eyes on the screen of his tablet.

Karp grunted and shrugged.

"He was born, he went to school, he joined the army, he got married, his wife died. That is all. Years and years of nothing. No jobs? No school reunions? He is invisible to me," Nestor said.

"Google him," Karp said.

"You think I didn't Google him? The first thing I did was Google him."

"Re-Google him."

"There is no such thing as re-Googling. It is not a slot machine, Karp. Same results every time."

Karp said nothing. He was eyeing an attendant who was showing off a lot of ass bending over a service cart. *I would Google that*, he thought to himself. *I would Google that until it bleeds*. He caught Nestor's disapproving glance.

"You should know this stuff, Karp. You should learn this stuff. What if there was a day when I was no longer here?" Nestor said.

"Then I would no longer be here, dear one. I would be dead as well," Karp said and squeezed Nestor's thigh with the same gentle touch that always surprised the younger man.

"Refresh those drinks?" the big-assed attendant said with a professional smile. His name tag read ANDY.

The plane arrived on time at Huntsville International. A man they knew from Detroit by way of Kiev joined them in the line for the bus out to the rental services. He had a FedEx package under his arm that he left behind when he got out at the stop for Budget. Karp picked it up off the seat and took it along when he and Nestor got out at Enterprise. The pair rented a car and drove out of the city to the apartment listed for Levon Edward Cade on the driver's license.

Karp drove while Nestor prized open the FedEx box. Inside was a pair of Browning automatics fully loaded with a spare magazine for each. There were two knives as well — a curved skinning knife in a leather sheath and a clasp knife with a four-inch blade. There was also a small pry bar that would fit in a pocket and a brand new pay-as-you-go cell phone charged with one thousand minutes.

Using the mini-pry bar, they were into the apartment within a second. The place showed all the signs of a man who lived alone except for the neatness. The place was dusted — no dishes or glasses in the sink. The bed was made, for God's sake. The bedroom was featureless except for a chest of drawers and a twin mattress on a platform.

Karp took the closet and Nestor the dresser.

The closet was all pressed casual or work clothes still in the plastic wrap from a cleaner. Karp sniffed and smelled gun oil. He uncovered a rifle and shotgun cleaning kit tucked behind a pair of Rubbermaid containers of neatly folded army fatigues in desert camo. He pulled the containers from the closet and felt the walls all around for panels — no hiding places for guns.

Nestor pulled drawers from the dresser and dumped them on the bed. Socks, briefs, t-shirts and running shorts. Some change fell to the floor and some of the coins sounded heavier than normal currency. Nestor crouched and picked up some colorful coins the size of silver dollars. They were decorated in gold and silver and enamel. One had a diving eagle on one side and a map of Afghanistan on the other. Another had Bart Simpson with a grinning skull face holding a bloody dagger in skeletal hands. They bore acronyms that meant nothing to Nestor except NCIS which he knew from television.

"He is military," Nestor said tossing a coin to Karp.

Karp laughed at the spooky Bart and stuck the coin in his pocket.

They went into the living room which was as spartan as the bedroom. A pair of cheap armchairs. A pressed wood end table and the last analog television in America. In place of a table and chairs near the kitchenette was an antique roll-top desk and wheeled office chair. These were the only interesting pieces of furniture in the apartment, the only evidence of any kind of the individuality of the occupant.

Nestor pried open the drawers and top to rifle the desk while Karp made sandwiches from the contents of the refrigerator. The younger man sat on a stool at the kitchen counter and went through paper files he found in the desk. Karp played homemaker placing sandwiches and beers between them. Swiss and hot mustard for the big man and peanut butter and jam for his little *tovarich*. Such an American Nestor had become.

"Bingo," Nestor said.

Karp grunted through a mouthful of sandwich.

"These are legal papers. Our man Levon is a father. He is suing his father-in-law in court for custody of his daughter," Nestor said.

"America," Karp said, spitting crumbs of bread and cheese as he spoke.

"This man was a soldier. You ask me, too smart to come back here. He must know that we know him now."

Karp nodded.

"Let us go see his father-in-law and see what we might learn."

"You are so smart, dear one," Karp said, reaching across the counter to give his partner a tender slap.

Nestor touched the streak of mustard on the bigger man's cheek.

They finished their sandwiches and left for the house in Twickenham.

34

Gunny Leffertz said:

"There's no reasoning with evil."

Levon filled a cart at a Walmart in Corinth, Mississippi.

He bought clothes for Merry that she helped pick out. Shirts, underwear, socks, jeans, and a heavier winter coat. Also a pair of boots and a sweater she "just had to have." A new toothbrush, a bottle of Flintstones vitamins, a comb, and some coloring books and crayons. A selection of her favorite breakfast cereals went into the cart. She had enough changes of clothes to last a week without laundering.

He paid with cash and the elderly woman at the register remarked that "someone is a very lucky little girl."

"And it's not even my birthday." Merry beamed.

They ate at a Subway before getting back on the highway south towards Tupelo.

Levon took a trio of pills from a plastic carrying case he kept in his pocket. He popped them in his mouth and swallowed with a sip of raspberry iced tea.

"Are you still sick?" Merry said.

"I'm not sick," he said.

"Grandpa says you are. He says you take pills because you're sick."

"These pills? They're like vitamins for my brain. I don't take them because I'm sick. I take them to make me think better."

"I'd like to think better."

"You think just fine, honey."

"Does your friend know we're coming?" Merry said, stabbing a straw into the ice for the last sip of punch at the bottom of the paper cup.

"He doesn't know."

"You should call him. We don't want to be rude."

"He doesn't have a phone, Merryberry."

She knitted her brows. No phone? Unthinkable. Everyone had a phone.

"Why not, Daddy?"

"Well, his wife and him live way out in the woods away from the world. They like it that way."

"Why's that?"

"My friend says he's seen everything in the world he wants to see. He headed back into the trees and built himself a cabin there."

"So, us coming to see him is a surprise?" she said.

"Something like that," Levon said.

Merry was silent for a while, stabbing at the ice in her drink cup with her straw.

"Daddy?" she said after a bit.

"Yes, honey?"

"You promised to take me to Disneyworld."

"Well, I can't do that right now."

"It's okay," she said. It was the opposite of okay, but she wanted him to know she was going to be brave about it. It was also important that he knew just *how* brave she was being. She slumped back into the booth as he gathered their sandwich papers to clear the table.

"Merry," he said standing and holding her coat out to her.

"Yes?" she said, being *so* very brave but not looking him in the face.

"Last time I was at my friend's, I saw wild ponies in the woods."

She snatched the coat from his hand and was heading for the store exit in her new boots. He trotted after.

Disneyworld?

Never heard of the place.

35

Dr. Roth heard the doorbell ring but chose to ignore it to finish his morning shave. He was patting his cheeks with cucumber infused witch hazel when he heard Marcia call his name. Her voice quavered like the time she found the garden snake under the water heater.

Dressed only in a bath towel tied around his waist he stepped to the top of the stairs. Down in the foyer, Marcia stood between two men who were dressed in dark leather coats. One of them had Marcia in a choke-hold. A gloved fist held a curved knife against his wife's side and angled to go up under her bottom rib. Jordan's vision was drawn to the tattoo on the man's neck. A grinning human skull smoking a cigarette.

The smaller of the two men, a young man with a baby face and hair to his shoulders, began to climb the stairs toward Jordan.

Jordan moved away down the hallway seeking options as he ran. The towel slipped down to his ankles tripping him. The doctor was back on his feet and sprinting for the end of the hall.

He owned no firearms. He'd read a study that proved that a gun in the home was 67% more likely to be used as a murder weapon than in an incident of home defense. The only phones, landlines, were downstairs in his office and the kitchen. A Danish study posited that cell and cordless phones significantly increased the risk of brain cancers. The Roths did not have an alarm system of any kind because Jordan saw it as a waste of funds as they'd spent so much to buy a home in a safe neighborhood.

Dr. Roth took the only alternative that remained for his continued survival.

He locked himself in the bathroom.

Braced against the sink cabinet, he listened to footsteps approaching on the hardwood floor. Cucumber infused sweat dripped from his face. The door between him and the invading strangers was a hollow fill door made of Masonite and recycled materials. It was part of the eco-friendly restoration of the house that Jordan insisted on before they moved in thirty years earlier. It would never stand up to whoever was in the hallway. The only window in the room was a double-glazed insulated window fixed in its frame with no opening options. It was only a matter of time before the door came down and they had him.

Jordan surprised the man in the hallway by pulling open the bathroom door.

The man stepped back raising a pistol of some kind at the naked doctor.

"I'm not resisting. There's no call for violence," Jordan said holding his palms out.

The long-haired young man's expression melted from surprise to a cruel leer. He used his gloved gun hand to brush the hair from his eyes.

When he saw this man's eyes the doctor reassessed

his decision to give in so easily and admitted it might not have been the wisest course. The eyes looked like he imagined a hawk's might when soaring high above the earth looking for prey.

"Say nothing more, or I shoot you. Come with me or I shoot you," the young man said in accented English.

"May I put on some clothes?" Jordan said.

The young man raised the gun to aim at the doctor's face.

Naked, Jordan led the way to the head of the steps with the young man following.

36

Hands bound with tape behind his back, Jordan Roth was packed into the confines of a car trunk where he lay pressed against Marcia's back. Still naked. He shivered in the cold while searching the invisible organ of his mind for a solution that would save their lives.

This had to be about Levon Cade, his son-in-law. What kind of trouble was he in? What had he done that brought these men to the door of the Roth home?

Marcia was crying and whispering incoherently. It was a prayer. The sound of it made it difficult for Jordan to concentrate on his thoughts.

"Please, please," he whispered and nudged her back with his knees.

She mistook it for an effort to comfort her and reduced the noises she made to intermittent whimpering.

They rode a long way. The doctor lost track of time but it seemed like a long drive with many turns. They came to rest a moment. A rhythmic metallic rattling. A garage door going up. The car started forward again.

The sound of the motor resonated now in echoes. They had pulled inside a building rather than a garage. The car stopped. The engine died. Two doors opened and slammed shut.

The trunk popped open. The young man and the brute were there. They hauled the Roths from the trunk and walked/dragged them over a concrete floor to a metal chair by a table. Jordan was placed in the chair. His wife dropped to the floor.

The building was a cavernous empty space — an industrial warehouse abandoned for many years. Stacks of debris were pushed against the wall. There was a tang of rust and oil in the air.

The brute busied himself taping Jordan securely in the chair. The glue tugged at his naked flesh. Jordan remained silent. He would not plead. He would not bargain. He would wait to see what these men wanted and then decide his course. This was the decision he'd come to on the ride to this forgotten place. They would set the conditions of the game. He would play their game and win. They were thugs with simple minds and simple motives. He was an educated man with an agile mind.

The objects on the table were cause for alarm. A battery-operated power drill. A hammer. A box of four-inch nails. A can of charcoal lighter. A pair of adjustable pliers.

The younger of the two leaned back on the table.

"Levon Cade is your son-in-law?" Nestor said.

"Yes. He was. Until my daughter died," Jordan said, voice level, eyes turned away from the tools on the table.

"Do you know where he is?"

"I do not know where—"

Nestor nodded.

Karp pulled the Browning from his waistband and shot Marcia twice through the head.

Jordan stared. First at his wife lying shrunken and dead still in a spreading lake of blood. Then into the predator eyes of the younger man.

"That is to show that we are serious. Continue to lie and believe me, you will envy your wife."

"But I don't know where he is. I'd tell you if I knew. I'd have told the police if I knew."

"Police?" Karp said, glancing at Nestor.

"What do you mean by police?" Nestor said, stepping from the table to lean close to Jordan's face.

Jordan began to speak. Nestor held up a hand.

"Wait. Wait. Wait."

Nestor took his tablet from an inside pocket of his coat. He poked and swiped. A voice speaking a foreign language came from the device. A gruff voice with a bass tone that was discernible even through the tinny speakers of the tablet. Nestor answered in the same language. A curt exchange followed.

The tablet was held up before the doctor's face. On the screen was the face of a hard-looking man of perhaps Jordan's age, maybe older or younger. The man locked eyes with Jordan over the link as intensely as if they were in the same room.

"You talk to police? Of what do you talk to police?"

"My son-in-law. He took my granddaughter without permission. I filed charges. I told the police all I knew."

"It's true. We saw the legal papers, *shef,*" Nestor said.

"You told police all you know. What is it you tell them?" the man on the tablet asked.

"That Cade is insane. He's dangerous. He suffers from PTSD. He's on psychotropic drugs, mood altering medications. He's capable of anything and he has my granddaughter with him." Jordan stated his case clearly. They both wanted the same thing. They could all be reasonable men.

"He is crazy. He is dangerous. This I know. Where is he? That is what I need from you," the tablet said.

"I don't know where he is. I told you that. I would tell you where he is if I knew."

"Will he call you? Will he be contacting you?"

"No. He hates me as much as I hate him. He won't call."

"Your granddaughter. Maybe she call?"

"She's nine years old. I'm not sure she remembers the house number."

"She have phone. All kids got phones."

"Not Meredith. I forbade her to have a cell phone." The doctor caught himself before making mention of the Danish studies.

"I believe you. You do not know. A liar would make up a story to tell me."

Jordan relaxed at the words. His muscles ached from the strain of the tension and the cold.

"Nestor?" the tablet said. Nestor held the tablet before him and there was a new exchange in what sounded like Russian now. Nestor tapped the screen, killing the call. He nodded to Karp.

Karp pulled his Browning once again.

Jordan was more irritated than surprised.

"You want to prove that you're idiots? You want to do the stupid thing? Then go ahead and kill me," the doctor said. He sounded impatient with them like they were stubborn children.

Nestor held a hand up to Karp. This was a first. Nestor had seen people in this same situation beg, pray, pass out, weep, and make all kinds of promises. He'd been offered drugs, money, cars, pussy, and blow jobs by others taped in chairs, suspended by their heels, or buried to their necks.

This is the first time he was ever scolded.

"We are stupid? We killed your wife. We have a gun to your head. But we're the idiots."

"Yes."

"You have balls, my man. Big ones. But who holds the gun?"

"You want Cade. I'm your only possible contact. The man is a classic loner. He has no family. No friends. If I'm gone, you lose any chance you would ever have had of finding him."

"You told us you don't know where he is."

"That doesn't mean that I can't find out. Given time to think about it, without the threat of pain or death, I would be able to help you locate him."

"You really hate his ass."

"He killed my daughter," Jordan said.

"Give me one more reason or my *tovarich* brings this to an end."

"I'm a doctor. A surgeon. Surely your people, your organization, the man on the tablet, would have use for a surgeon now and then."

Nestor glanced at Karp then back at the doctor.

"You can write prescriptions?"

"Whatever you're looking for. Whatever amounts you need. I'm on the board at Huntsville and Crestwood."

Nestor shrugged and reached out to pat Karp's gun hand. The brute returned the Browning to his waistband. Nestor cut the tape holding the doctor to the chair with his clasp knife. Together they carried/dragged the doctor to the car and placed him in the back seat. Marcia went into the trunk along with the sack of tools from the table. The pair settled back in the front seat.

"We're taking you home to get some clothes and your prescription pad. Then we get something to eat. How's that sound to you?" Nestor said, turned in the seat to speak to Jordan.

"Yes. Could you turn the heat up, please?" the doctor said.

Karp cranked up the fan and warm air washed over Jordan. He allowed his body to unknot from the tension built up over the past hours. He fell asleep as they drove, awakened once when the corpse in the trunk rocked against the wall behind the backseat. The doctor fell back into a doze, his invisible organ free to dream of warm streams and green grass under a summer sun.

37

Gunny Leffertz said:

"The older I get, the more I know that the rarest thing in the world is having someone who honestly, truly, and purely gives a shit about you."

They were a half hour off the county road and following a switchback coursing around hills covered in white birch. Levon slowed to a stop twice to allow deer to cross the road.

He turned the truck onto a driveway marked with a battered mailbox with a faded Marine Corps eagle, globe and anchor painted on it. The driveway had a hard-packed stone surface. It snaked alongside a dry wash to ford a shallow creek fringed with winter ice as thin as lace.

A fringe of tall pines acted like a gateway either side of the roadway. A one-level log cabin was visible ahead. White smoke curled from the wide chimney of stacked stone. A Dodge Ram sat high on lifts and knobby tires in the gravel yard before the house. A waxed-shiny Range Rover was in the shade of a carport on a concrete hard-stand. In the center of the yard was a walled flower bed, empty but for a flagpole atop of which an American flag fluttered above a smaller USMC flag.

A man stood on the deep porch that ran across the face of the cabin. He came down the steps with a double-barrel shotgun cradled easily in his arms. A black man with steel gray hair cropped close. He had massive shoulders and a thick neck visible under a denim farm coat. His eyes were hidden behind dark wraparounds. Beneath the glasses was a scowl that looked as if it were frozen there for all time. He walked out to meet the approach of the Avalanche.

“Hope it’s okay I stopped by like this,” Levon said stepping onto the gravel.

“Knew you were comin’. Heard you pulling off the county road.” The man’s scowl deepened.

“Couldn’t be the motion alarm a mile back helped, you lying bastard.”

Merry stood by the truck, looking between the men uncomprehending.

The man with the shotgun’s scowl vanished into a broad smile of welcome.

"About time you come to visit me, Cade. Who'd you bring with you?"

“My little girl. Merry.”

“Well, I’m anxious to meet the little princess your daddy talks about all the time.”

“My daddy talks to you about me?” Merry skipped

around the truck to take the man's offered hand. He held it out waiting for her to take it.

"All the time, sweetie-pie." The man pulled her close in a tight hug. He smelled like fresh cut wood and cinnamon.

"Honey, I want you to meet Gunny Leffertz," Levon said.

38

Dinner was pasta and venison sausage in a marinara followed by freshly baked apple pie. Coffee for the grown-ups and creamy tea for Merry.

The cabin was like something out of a fairy tale to Merry. The great room had high ceilings with open beams. The fireplace of river stone was big enough for her to walk into without stooping. A big Irish wolfhound slept on a rough weave carpet before the hearth. The kitchen came off the great room as did the bedrooms and two bathrooms. She helped Joyce, Gunny's wife, clear the table.

Joyce was as nice to her as Gunny was. She talked to Merry as they washed and dried the dishes together. She told Merry that she met Gunny in Hawaii a long time ago when they were both in the Marines. When Gunny lost his eyesight and retired, she retired too, and they got married and they built this cabin in the Mississippi woods.

"Gunny can't see?" Merry said.

"Blind as an old bat," Joyce said.

"But he doesn't use a cane or bump into things."

"That's because we've lived here long enough that he knows where everything is. He even fools me sometimes. But you take him down to Tupelo and he'll walk right in front of a bus."

Joyce laughed. Merry joined her.

"Was he hurt being a soldier?" Merry said becoming grave all of a sudden.

"Marine, honey. Never call a Marine a soldier."

"No, ma'am. Sorry, ma'am."

"Well old Gunny got a piece of steel in his head from a roadside bomb back in—Are you sure you want to hear this?"

Merry nodded with enthusiasm.

"Back in Desert Storm. A piece of metal no bigger than a pin. And it was in a place where doctors couldn't get to it. Over the years, and because Gunny wouldn't take it easy like they told him to, the piece of metal moved to press on some nerves, and he lost his sight over time."

"My daddy never talks about when he was fighting."

"Some daddies don't."

"He met Gunny back then? They became friends?"

"Gunny was a teacher at a very special school your father went to. Gunny says Levon Cade was the best student he ever had."

"What did Gunny teach him?"

"You'd better ask your daddy that," Joyce said, putting away the last dried plate into a cabinet.

Merry nodded. She would ask him.

Levon and Gunny sat out on the front porch listening to the trees creak in the wind. They were sharing some high-grade lightning made by a neighbor.

"What kind of trouble you in, Slick?" Gunny said.

"Why do you think I'm in trouble?"

"This man can't see. Don't mean this man is blind. You bring your little one up here out of the clear blue. She's packed to stay but you're not. You want to keep lying to your old gunny?"

"Wasn't lying. I only wanted to know how you smelled trouble."

"You stink of it, Slick. Now tell me a story." Gunny settled back in his chair.

Levon gave him the long and short of it. When he stopped talking, Gunny had some questions.

"These Russians. How big is their outfit? What's their reach?" he said.

"They're not *mafia*. The Vor gangs are smaller. Like the *plazas* the Mexican cartels authorize. They're connected but not that high up."

"How far up the chain are you going to have to go?"

"That's up to them, isn't it? I need to find their command and control and either get a promise from them or take them out," Levon said.

"Promises ain't worth shit from anyone. You leave one of them alive and you're gonna be hidin' for a long time," Gunny said.

"Me and Merry are going to be our own witness protection. I don't want that life for her, but I don't know what else to do."

"Your little one okay with staying here a while?"

"I told her there were wild ponies."

"I mean she okay with you going away and her stayin' with Joyce and me?"

"I'll stay till tomorrow night. Give her some time to get used to it. Hearing the two of them giggling in the kitchen, I think she's ready to adopt Joyce as a grandma anyway. Might not even miss me."

"Bullshit," Gunny said.

They sipped the hard corn liquor. There was an aftertaste of apples once the fire died down.

"I need some ordnance," Levon said after a while.

"We'll have a look in the morning. You take anything you like."

"I can pay for it."

"And if you try to, you'll be pickin' that cash out of your ass." Gunny turned to Levon with his badass stare that still worked even if the old Marine was stone blind.

39

Gunny Leffertz said:

"You can never have enough gun."

He was naked and hurting and cold.

"Have you had time to think, Dimi?"

The voice was tinny and flat.

Dimi came fully awake in an ice-cold drizzle.

Tupo was standing over him, pouring a bottle of beer over him. Yvan was by him holding his hand out. In his fingers was a smartphone held up for Dimi to see. Uncle Symon's tiny face glared at him from the screen.

"Dimi. Have you had time to think?"

Think? It was all Dimi could to do to keep from passing out again. His ears rang. His vision spun. Every beat of his heart brought a new tide of pain to his skull.

He'd lost his room privileges. He lay in the musty straw of the stable set. Manacles were around his ankles and secured to a long chain slung over a ceiling joist. The gear was part of the bondage stuff left behind by the recent lessees. Before leashing him like a dog, Tupo and Yvan made him take his clothes off. He refused at first, certain they were going to ass-rape him, these sick prison fucks. Tupo pressed the barrel of a gun to his head. Dimi shucked out of his clothes.

They chained him. They gave him a beating. No malice. No questions. They took turns. Just following orders. All part of the job.

Tupo gave Dimi a shot to the gut that loosened his bowels. A stream of bloody shit sprayed over his legs. They dropped him to the straw then and went back to their card table.

Uncle Symon had left before the stripping and chaining and beating. Now his uncle was back. Virtually, anyway.

"Get him up," Uncle Symon said.

Tupo and Yvan lifted Dimi and dropped him in a chair. Tupo handed him what was left of the beer. Dimi sipped, struggling to keep it down.

"Have you had time to think, Dimi?" Symon said from the phone.

"I told you, Uncle. Maybe the bikers know."

"We spoke to them. They do not know the man. He is a stranger to them. I believe them."

"I swear to Christ I don't know either," Dimi said. Tears started in his eyes. His throat closed with the effort not to sob.

"Something at Skip's. You know. Skip's."

"The place in Tampa? I know it."

"This man Cade killed our people at Skip's. Robbed us. This was before he killed your father."

Dimi licked his lips and nodded.

"Did you sell drugs there? Did you make trouble there with someone, Dimi?"

"I told you and told you and told you, Uncle. I don't sell drugs anywhere. I'm not a dealer. I'm a wholesaler. Why can't you understand that?"

"Hit him," the face on the phone said.

Tupo slammed a fist into Dimi's face. Dimi heard a wet snap. He tasted blood in his mouth.

"Again. Just to hurt."

Tupo slapped Dimi across the ear with an open hand. Dimi couldn't believe, even after the beating the night before, how much it hurt. An explosion inside his head followed by a dagger of pain from his ear. A high whistling sound drowned out everything for a long moment.

"Enough." Symon sighed.

Tupo stepped back. The assault via Skype was on pause for now.

"You are not telling me the truth. You think that lying will keep you alive," Symon said inches from his face.

Dimi stared at the fuzzy image filling his field of vision.

"You are a man because you can take a beating. Then we show you that you are no man. We treat you like a bitch."

Dimi watched Yvan hand the smartphone over to Tupo who held it close to Dimi's face. Yvan walked away and returned a moment later with a push broom. He snapped the broom handle over his knee, leaving a two-foot section in one fist.

Yvan spat on the end and grinned.

The world pixilated and then went red and then black.

Dimi was offline.

40

"Jesus Palomino, Gunny," Levon said in a whisper.

They were in a block-walled building set into a hillside well behind the cabin. Accessible by a hard-packed walkway and enclosed by a cyclone cage. Gunny hit the combination on the keypad flawlessly. He swung the heavy steel door open to let them in.

The familiar smell of gun oil and Cosmoline. Fluorescents in the ceiling winked on. The room was ten by ten and lined with racks of weapons in protective sleeves. Above the racks were shelves of ammo boxes. The back wall was stacked with cases in wood and high-impact plastic.

"This room is some kind of prepper's dream," Levon said unsheathing a government model Thompson submachine gun in pristine condition.

"Preppers. Screwballs, I call 'em. Got a pack of 'em over the hill diggin' out their half-assed bunker on weekends instead of golfing or barbecuing."

"So, why do you have all this shock and awe in your backyard?"

“Just an old jarhead who can’t sleep right without some strike capability handy,” Gunny said smiling.

“You have anything newer than Iwo Jima?”

“Fuck you, Slick. I got whatever the hell you need to get you out of whatever corner you’re in. What are you looking for?”

"A long gun. Something for range and a good scope that's not fiddly. A rifle, an M4, without all the after-market bullshit. And two handguns. One for serious work and the other for a hideout."

“Let’s go shopping.” Gunny grinned and ran his fingers along the racked rifles and shotguns.

Levon picked out a cut-down M-4 with a heavy rubberized forestock. Gunny told him it had a reinforced action and worked as smooth as a duck’s ass. For the long gun, he stayed with the classics: a Winchester Model 70 in a Rynex stock. The handgun choices were a Sig Sauer 9 mm and a hammerless Colt snubbie in .38 special, both in stainless.

“These are all off the books?” Levon said.

“Hell, not only are they not here now, they never was anywhere,” Gunny said, pulling down fresh boxes of ammo and magazines for the Mike and Sig.

Before they were done Gunny insisted Levon take a shotgun, a cut-down Mossberg Mariner with a pistol grip.

“Nobody was ever sorry they brought one of these along,” Gunny said.

“You know you’re not getting any of these back, Gunny,” Levon said.

“I’m countin’ on it. You use ’em and lose ’em. Just bring your ass back here to your little one.”

“I think I have what I need here.”

“How about a few bricks of C-4, Slick?”

"I wouldn't say no."

They made four trips from the arsenal to the gravel lot in front of the cabin. Levon dropped the tailgate of the Avalanche.

"You can't take the truck you came here in. You drove it up from Tampa. They'll have the plates," Gunny said.

"I'll switch plates somewhere on the road." Levon lifted two plastic ammo cases up onto the gate. Gunny put his hand on Levon's wrist.

"You'll take our Range Rover. She's old but she runs good. You switch plates on her and you're in stealth mode again."

"Can't do that."

"You will or you ain't leaving here."

"You were never able to keep me any place I didn't want to be, Gunny."

"That hurts. That's cold, Slick."

Gunny's smile broadened as his grip on Levon's wrist tightened.

"All right. I'll take the Rover. Joyce won't mind?"

"She won't."

A final squeeze and Gunny released Levon's wrist.

They loaded the Rover and went inside the cabin for breakfast.

41

"The girl. It has to be the girl," Dimi said to the phone held before him.

"What girl? Who is this girl?" Uncle Symon's face filled the screen.

"A girl. I was in Skip's. College girl."

"All of this for some bitch? What is this bullshit?"

"The police came looking for her. They came to Skip's. They learned nothing."

The image on the screen shifted then settled. Uncle Symon's dark eyes studied Dimi's face across the space that separated them. The secret to Dimi's entire future was in those eyes.

"What do the police know, Dimi?"

"Nothing! No one told them anything. Not a fucking word, uncle."

"Who was this bitch? Who would come looking for her?"

"I have all of that. I mean, I can get it. I sold her driver's license and credit cards. I can tell you who."

Dimi gave the name and location. Symon wrote them down then broke the connection, cutting off his nephew as the man began to plead to be released.

Symon selected a cell phone from the row on his desk and called Karp and Nestor.

42

Gunny Leffertz said:

"Get all the intel you can. Intel is good. Even bad intel has some worth. Every lie has some truth in it. You need to learn the difference."

There was something liberating about it all.

Dr. Roth rode back home in the back seat with Marcia's body in the trunk. The two men removed him from the car, the smaller man holding his elbow to help him into the house. The larger man hefted Marcia from the trunk and carried her up to the porch and inside.

It was all so unreal. He was naked in broad daylight. His wife was being brought home with half her skull missing. Over the border hedge in the front yard, he could hear a neighbor's leaf blower whining. Children shouted at play somewhere down the street. High overhead, the contrail of a commercial jet cut the sky in half.

All around, life went on even as Jordan Roth's world teetered at the edge of oblivion.

The smaller man kept watch on Jordan while he pulled on clothing and packed three more changes into an overnight bag with no attention to coordination.

"Your pad?" the smaller man asked holding out a hand for the zippered bag.

"In my office."

The smaller man gestured, and Jordan led the way downstairs. There was a sharp chemical smell in the air. Gasoline. Coming from the cellar.

The larger man rejoined them as they were leaving the office. He had three dark bottles cradled in one arm. He'd been in the cellar. Jordan was curious as to what vintages the man chose to take. They exited the house together. Jordan was allowed to sit in the back seat. His bag went in the trunk.

He looked from the rear window of the car as they backed down the driveway to the street. A fog of smoke was rising from the basement window wells. A fire.

A pyre for Marcia.

They left the Roths' now-former address, and the tony neighborhood they'd called home for thirty years, for a golden strip lined with shopping marts, car dealerships, and standalone stores.

The car made its way east in fits and starts, stopping at every Walgreens, CVS, Target and Walmart. The car would park in the fire lane while the doctor would write a prescription for various Schedule Three drugs. Tylox, Oxycontin, Empirin, Fiorinal, Ativan, Halcion, Librium, Valium, Xanax, Amytal, Nembutal, and others in generic and brand names. His captors were knowledgeable of doses and legal prescription amounts.

The two men took turns entering the drug stores and

returning to the car after fifteen and twenty-minute waits. The big man did not want to talk but Jordan found the smaller of the two a willing conversationalist.

The smaller man, the pretty boy with the predator's eyes, explained that they were using a collection of credit cards under various names to make the purchases. So, the pick-ups were essentially free to them. A fortune in forbidden prescriptive narcotics and depressants worth many times their market value in the right places. This was all a bonus above what they were being paid for their current assignment.

The doctor wasn't certain if they meant to keep him alive for his surgical skills or merely until his prescription pad was empty. This couldn't go on for long. Even now the fire would have been discovered. Jordan and Marcia Roth would be feared dead in the fire. Was there an apparatus to shut down his status as a qualified scrip writer once it was determined that he was either missing or deceased?

He took some comfort from them allowing him to pack a bag with a few days' worth of clothes. Of course, they might have done this to give him a false sense of his own security to make him compliant. These were heartless men, ruthless men. But they were professionals. Their every action branded them as such. In that way, he felt a kinship with them: men skilled at an unpleasant task that required certain skills and a high level of expert detachment to perform, like killing a fellow human being or sawing into the skull of a living subject.

They were parked in front of a Target. Jordan sat quietly in the back seat with the bigger man munching a protein bar behind the wheel. The smaller man exited hurriedly and took the passenger seat. He spoke to the driver in Russian. A brief exchange followed. The big man nodded his head toward the doctor.

Jordan held his breath.

"Find a motel," the smaller man said.

Jordan exhaled.

They were keeping him for now.

43

Tobias Garrett shanked his ball into the trees. He muttered a curse as he started to hike after it.

"Rotten luck," a member of his party called after him in accented English.

He was handicapping himself so as not to show up his guests. They were piss-poor golfers, but he dearly wanted their business. No trouble falling on his ass a few times to give them the win if it meant getting the fat contract they offered.

His cell tingled in his pocket as he was using his driver to part the ferns in search of his little white Titleist. It wasn't a number he recognized.

"Garrett. Lone Star Solutions. How can I make your world a safer place?"

"That shrapnel still giving you a hitch in your getalong?"

Levon Cade. Holy shit. Cade was identifying himself using a reference from a shared adventure in Manila. An RPG brought down their chopper. Garrett remembered little after that except that Cade was always there, always by him, until they were safely back aboard the *Stennis*.

"Only in the cold weather, brother."

"Can we talk, Tobey?"

"This is a business line. I can call you back in two hours. The number on my display good for you?"

"Yeah. For a few days. Talk to you then."

The call ended.

Tobias hacked away at the ball to free it from the rough, taking four swings, and still came to the green one point behind the best player in his foursome. Arabs were shit at golf. Tobias sank the putt to take the hole.

44

Gunny Leffertz said:

"You have to know more about your enemy than he knows about you. That means keeping your ass hid while you study his. That means limiting your encounters with him. The more times you fight the more he learns about your moves. Make the first fight the last fight whenever you can. Find him. Fuck him. And forget him."

Levon pulled in at truck stops along the way back to Tampa. He collected throwaway cell phones, paying cash every time for the phones and calling cards.

The parting from Merry had been hard. It might have been better if she'd cried. She held it back, not letting him see how his leaving was tearing her up. He looked back once in the rearview. Merry turned to bury her head in Joyce's shoulder. Gunny stood by waving.

A cell buzzed and lit up on the console by him. It was the phone he'd assigned to Tobey Garrett. He touched the tab on his earbud cord.

"Thanks for getting back to me. We're secure."

"Am I going to have to throw this phone in the lake after I hang up?"

"You might have to find a volcano to drop it into."

"Shit," Tobey hissed in his ear.

"I need intel. You're private sector now. Is that going to be a problem?"

"I still have my resources. It's what I trade on. What do you need?"

"A gang in Tampa. Family name Kolisnyk. K-O-L-I-S-N-Y-K. They go by Collins too. Not sure if that's a legal name change."

"Shit fuck, Cade. These are Russians?"

"Ukrainian. Same difference."

"Mafia or Vor?"

"They're Vor."

"You caught a small break, brother. They might wait to cut your balls off until *after* you're dead. How can I help you?"

"The usual. A way in. A profile. Holdings. History. Organization, Associations. Broad strokes."

"You working private sector yourself? Is this freelance?"

"One-time thing. I'm not printing business cards."

"Where have I heard that before? I don't need to know anything else to know that you're in over your head."

"Can you do it, Tobey?"

"Give me until ten tonight. I'm in Austin. I'll call you at this number."

"I appreciate it."

"Think of it as a portion of the down payment on all I owe you, brother."

The call ended. Levon continued south on US 65.

Levon was pulled in to refuel the Rover an hour north of Tallahassee when Tobey called back with the goods. The traffic on US 10 was a river of light in the dark beyond the blinking glow of the fluorescents over the pump stations. Levon sat in the front seat and took notes on a pad as Tobey spoke. He filled five pages before they were done.

"That enough?" Tobey said.

"It's all I needed."

"You're fucking with the wrong guys. Whatever you're into, they're not going to forget about you."

"I know how to hide."

"That's harder when you're alone. It's expensive too. You have a kid, right? You thought of her?"

"It's gone too far along for that."

"Shit, brother."

"It is what it is, Tobey."

"If you need money, you let me know. Hell, you live through this and need a job you let me know."

"I'll be in contact about some fresh paper. The works."

"It's yours. Good luck."

The line went dead.

Levon pulled to the back of the lot where the semis were parked. He lay down in the back seat as best he could and slept until just before dawn.

45

The dog was barking.

Delia Wiley elbowed her husband.

"Your dog's barking."

Joe Bob awakened. It was his dog when it barked or shit on the rug. He grunted and fell back to sleep.

"Still barking." She nudged him again.

"Damn it," he huffed, sitting up.

Joe Bob sat up in the king-sized bed, listening. Mojo was sure barking at something. Deer crossing the property. The neighbor on the next lot coming home late. Maybe someone poaching firewood off the sixty-acre conservation area that ringed the subdivision. Hoopies from the trailer park over by the county road started doing that every year when the weather turned cold.

Out in his fenced-in run Mojo went silent.

"He stopped. Deer probably," Joe Bob said.

His wife moaned in the affirmative. They were back to sleep in moments.

Something nudged Joe Bob. Something hard pressed

down into his shoulder. He grunted. It pressed again. Wrong side of the bed for Delia.

Joe Bob opened his eyes to see a big man standing over him. The man wore a black mask that covered his face. The man was pulling back the black pistol he'd used to prod Joe Bob awake. The man motioned for Joe Bob to sit up. Joe Bob saw that a smaller man, also in a mask, was on the bed straddling Delia and holding a pistol to her head. The smaller man nodded in greeting to Joe Bob.

The big man helped Joe Bob to his feet then shoved him into a padded chair in the corner of the room. The smaller man had Delia out of bed. She was mewling wordlessly. Joe Bob thought she was praying. The smaller man shoved her to the floor at Joe Bob's feet. She was whispering his name over and over again.

"Joe Bob? Joe Bob? Joe Bob?"

The smaller man took a seat on the corner of the bed. The gun in his gloved fist at rest on his leg.

"You know this man, Levon Cade?" Nestor said.

Joe Bob nodded. "He used to work for me."

The smaller man shook his head lazily.

"He still works for you. You gave him a new job," Nestor said.

"Okay," Joe Bob said.

"You will tell him to stop this job you gave him. You will tell him to come home. When he has come home you will call us," Nestor said. He plucked a strip of paper from the pocket of his leather jacket. He held it out for Joe Bob.

Joe Bob took the paper. It had a ten-digit number hand printed on it.

"You understand? You tell him to stop working and

come back home. You changed your mind. Okay? You understand what will happen unless you do this."

Joe Bob nodded.

"Good," Nestor said patting his knees before standing up. The two men walked for the door of the master bedroom.

"Sorry for the dog," Karp said before stepping into the dark hallway.

Joe Bob fell to his knees on the carpet. He drew his wife to him and held her close, whispering assurances in her ear.

"Are they the men who took Jenna?" she said, breaking from his grasp.

Joe Bob stared at her, features drained of blood.

Jenna. In the face of his own death, he'd forgotten Jenna.

46

Gunny Leffertz said:

"Only one person hates a coward more than me, and that's God Almighty Himself."

Merry leaned on the table and waved her hand before Gunny's eyes. He was teaching her to play chess at the kitchen table.

"What are you doing?" Gunny said.

"Nothing," she said and sat down.

"You don't believe I'm really blind?"

"I believe you."

"Then why were you waving your little hand in front of my face?"

"How do you know that if you can't see?" she said.

"Why do you think I can see?" he said fingering the crenulations atop the rook to his right.

"You beat me three games without being able to see."

"Maybe you're so bad at this game even a blind man can beat you."

"Unh-uh!"

"I know what a chess board looks like. I know how the pieces move. You let me know which piece you moved, and I can see it in my head."

"You 'member it?" she said in open awe.

"It's not hard. Memory is a muscle. The more you work it the stronger it gets. Your move, little girl."

"Did you teach my daddy chess? He told me you were his teacher," she said and slid a pawn forward with his hand atop hers.

"I taught him all kinds of things. Chess was not one of them. He's a good player though. Surprised he hasn't taught you already," he said, moving a pawn forward to block her path while freeing his bishop to move.

"What kind of school was it?"

"A very special school. A very hard school. My job was to teach men how to be smart even when they were hurt or scared or tired."

"You scared my daddy?" She pulled her hand from under his.

"Not so's you'd know it," he said and left his hand hovering over the mane of the knight until she slid her hand to the piece once more and moved it to threaten his queen.

"Your daddy was my best student. He taught me as much as I taught him. You want to hear a story about your daddy?"

"Mm-hm."

"We had your daddy locked up in a kind of jail. He had a secret, and his orders were not to tell us his secret. No matter how hungry or tired or thirsty he got. It was like a game, you see. Only after a few days it doesn't feel like a game anymore. Most men hold out a week or maybe two. You know what your daddy did?"

"Unh-uh."

"He escaped the first night. We locked him up and the next morning he was gone. And so was one of our trucks. And he took parts from all the other trucks so we couldn't chase him. He broke our radio so we couldn't call out for help. There we were, a whole school full of soldiers and marines stuck in the middle of nowhere with no way out and no way to tell anyone the trouble we were in."

"Wow."

"You bet wow. You know what happened next?"

"Unh-uh."

"Your daddy drove back the next day with a box of Mexican takeout. Must have driven all night and all day back and forth to the closest town."

"Was he in trouble?"

"Hell, no. He did what he was supposed to. He kept his secret. Only maybe four other men made it through my class without giving up his secret. Your daddy is the only one who ever escaped on me."

"Are you best friends, Gunny?"

"We're brothers, little girl. You know what that makes me?"

"No?"

"Your uncle."

"Cool," she said, and he felt her hand slide a bishop across the board to take his queen.

"I did not see that coming," Uncle Gunny said.

47

Joe Bob was freaking.

All alone in the shower, mud streaming from his legs, he was quietly falling apart. The mud was from digging a grave for Mojo in the early morning hours. The dog's skull was crushed. The Rottweiler weighed in at sixty pounds and needed a big hole.

He sank to the floor, face in hands, and let the needle spray of scalding water beat down on him. He let himself cry. He allowed the pain welling up in his chest to come out in a bestial wail. The all-around glass walls misted to hide him from the world.

Delia was already gone. She'd packed two bags and took off for her sister's place in Tulsa. She wasn't staying in this house one more night. If he believed her, she might never come back. Delia demanded he pay for a charter and Joe Bob didn't argue. Twenty grand for a deadhead flight to Oklahoma. He paid for that and the car that came and picked her up and took her away.

Joe Bob ran through his own options for heading for cover. He had responsibilities, people who relied on him, obligations. None of that meant anything if those two men came back.

And now he had to run.

There was no way to call off what he started when he called Levon Cade into his office.

He phoned Levon on the only number he had. He left messages until the voice mail was full.

Joe Bob didn't know what Levon had done that brought those men into his home. He only asked Levon to find his daughter. He never asked how that would be accomplished. It hadn't mattered to Joe Bob then. It sure as shit mattered now.

The men who came to see him knew why Levon was in Florida. They knew about Jenna. They knew where she was. They knew what happened to her. They were the ones Levon went to find. They offered him no solace, no answers, no hope of ever seeing Jenna again. All they did was promise that they would return if the search for Jenna continued.

That scared him. With the fright came shame. A father's shame at his own helplessness to help his child. A man couldn't turn from his flesh and blood to save his own skin. No man does that.

He raised his face to the spray and let the water wash his tears away then stood up and turned off the taps.

Joe Bob made up his mind. He wasn't running and he wasn't calling off what he'd started even if he could. Fuck these assholes. He'd unleashed Levon Cade on them, and they'd have to deal with that. He hadn't started this shit. They had. Whatever kind of hell Cade was raising down in Florida, they'd called it down on themselves.

Sometimes doing nothing at all is the best revenge.

48

Gunny Leffertz said:

"Like Ty Cobb said, 'Hit 'em where they ain't.'"

It was a matter of trust, Dr. Jordan Roth told himself as he sat gagged with his wrists duct taped to the hanging bar of a closet in room twenty-seven of the Golden Chariot Motor Lodge.

He thought he had an understanding with the two men who had taken him from the shelter of his old life and into a world of movement and chaos. They were accomplices now. He had cooperated with them willingly and with no resistance. But they insisted on treating him like a captive, like a child, still.

Something made them stop their pharmaceutical shopping spree. They quickly found a motel where they could pull their car directly up to the room. The place was run down, a hideous remnant of the '50s. Loud music was playing from one of the rooms that was being used to house a party. They'd deposited him here in the closet and left.

His hands were tingling from blood loss. He tried shifting in the tight confines of the closet but found no relief. His legs were tired. His feet hurt from standing. But if he relaxed, then his weight pulled the tape tight on his wrists and brought new pain.

The music and shouting and breaking glass stopped after a few hours. A strip of light beneath the closet door turned from watery blue to muted white as the sun filtered through the blinds over the windows in the bedroom outside.

A knock at the door followed by another. The jangle of a key ring, the turning of a lock. Someone was in the room, and it wasn't his captors. Lights were turned on outlining the closet door in a corona of yellow radiance. Water ran in the bathroom. A vacuum cleaner droned. A shadow grew to block the strip of light on the floor. The closet door swung open.

A diminutive woman in an oversized smock raised her eyebrows in mild shock. She was a Latina with almond eyes that regarded him without interest. He made mewling noises at her through the tape. Her only response was a sad shake of her head.

She reached up past him to retrieve a pair of fresh toilet paper rolls from the shelf above his head. After a prim nod, she turned away and shut the door.

The wheels of the vacuum cleaner squeaked away. The lights went out. The door closed and the lock snapped back in place.

He was alone again.

The doctor was awakened by noises from the room. The door opened and the big man was there. Jordan was cut free. They had McDonald's breakfast takeout. He drank two cups of orange juice and wolfed down a greasy egg and bacon sandwich.

"Take a shower. We are leaving here," the younger one with the pop star looks and predator eyes said when they were done eating.

The two men were taking him with them. It sounded like a long drive ahead.

They'd decided to keep him. He rushed to the bathroom to take his shower. The days ahead held adventures for him unimagined.

49

An explosion at a pawnshop in Seffner, a blue collar/no collar town south of Tampa, reduced the building to a scorched shell. It went boom at 3:00 am. A standalone store, the only outside damage was a spray of glass on the street before it.

The first suspect was a gas explosion. One of the firemen hosing down the smoldering wreckage called bullshit on that. He'd done three deployments in Iraq and knew the stink of discharged C-4 when he smelled it. Someone was pissed at somebody and letting them know it.

Just in case somebody missed the point, a second pawn shop, this one in Port Richey north of Tampa exploded. Another standalone blasted hollow within twenty minutes of the first explosion.

The following morning, Symon Kharchenko received a FedEx package addressed to him at his condo. Inside was a cellphone with a note on a Post-It in marker.

CALL ME.

Symon hit send.

"Yeah." A male voice. An American.

"You have balls, my friend. I tell you that," Symon said. He paced the great room of the condo.

"You know what I want. Give me the girl and this ends."

"This is never going to end. Not for you. We know who you are."

"And I know who you are, Kharchenko. I know what you have. I know how to take it away."

"You have already taken my sons."

"Give me the girl and this ends. Keep this phone so you can tell me when you have her."

"You give me orders? Tell me what to do? Fuck your mother!" This last was shouted in Ukrainian as Symon strode out onto his balcony and sent the phone flying out into space to fall into the water of the marina many stories below.

It was still early morning. He was dressed in a silk robe only. His own house phone rang. He snatched it from his dresser. It was Soshi with the latest he'd heard. The Georgian had special contacts inside the county sheriff departments where the two pawnshops once stood. Both were brought down by strategically placed charges. Officially the motive was robbery and the blasts were meant to cover any evidence.

"Robbery?" Symon said.

"The under-counter safes are both gone. Torn out and carried away," Soshi said.

Together over a million dollars in cash at least.

Both pawnshops were money laundries for the Vor. It was easy to move ill-gotten cash through a shop that bought and sold items using cash, items that were all aftermarket. The meticulously kept sales records of each store were almost entirely fiction. On paper, there were ongoing concerns. In reality, the only car on the lots most days belonged to each shop's manager.

They were separately owned through two different holding companies with no connection to one another. Even the managers and paper-only owners, of each shop had no idea their businesses were connected in any way. This Levon Cade knew they were connected and struck at them to send a message. He knew more about the brotherhood's operations than they knew about him.

"He has no family but a young daughter, and she has disappeared," Symon said.

"The man is alone? What man is alone?" Soshi said.

Symon did not tell the fat Georgian about the missing girl and her building contractor father who'd paid this Cade to find her. Soshi would be on the phone to everyone. There was no need for all to know what had brought this curse upon them. And the father-in-law. Symon needed to think on that one.

"We should give Cade's name to the police. Let them find him," Soshi said.

"No. We will not do that. That is not our way," Symon said.

"How do we find him?"

"We are many. He is one."

"Exactly, Symon. How do we find one man in a city? It is like finding one louse in your bed. Remember the lice in the camps?"

Symon grunted that he did.

"This man knows where to strike us, how to hurt us. We can use all our men to look for him and leave our interests unguarded."

"Then what do I do, Soshi?"

"Give him what he wants and be rid of him."

"And let Danya and Vanko's deaths go unanswered," Symon said.

"Give him Dimi. It is Dimi who brought this on us. Let Dimi pay for all."

Symon ended the call without a farewell.

50

The driver stood well away from his semi as the gantry lowered the Conex over his truck bed. The sun was warm but the wind off the bay waters had a chilling effect on the Port of Tampa. The driver was not used to this kind of cold. Florida was supposed to be warm, *hermano*.

He was up from Honduras with papers that identified him as a fully licensed transport driver named Isaac Birnbaum of Circe, Arkansas. He worked for Don White Freight. He didn't know who Don White was. He didn't know Don White was a total fiction created as the founder for a company owned by Bayside Transit through a Delaware corporation called Morgantown Trucking and all of those bodies were a part of Stoneforge Ltd., a closely held limited partnership in which all the partners were named Yuri Baghdasarian, a member of the same Vor brotherhood as the Kharchenkos and Kolisnyks.

The container inched lower and lower onto the chassis until it was in place and secured.

The import manifest described the contents of the container as organic fertilizer. According to its paperwork, the forty-foot cargo container was filled with stacks of bagged primo cattle feces from Brazil.

In truth, the steel box was packed floor to ceiling, back to front, with cases of counterfeit Marlboros from China. Manufactured in a hidden factory in rural and remote Yunxiao, each pack cost under twenty cents to produce. Even with shipping, bribes and distribution, there was a 2000% profit to be made. And the profits got sweeter the further north the cigarettes traveled. The taxes on a carton of butts rose astronomically depending on where the truck wound up. The contents of the container on Isaac Birnbaum's truck were worth $20 million dollars in New York.

The truck pulled away from the gantry area and made its way around to the checkpoint where it stopped for radiation scanning as ordered by Homeland Security. Isaac's paperwork was glanced at by a customs agent and waved through. The load of Fauxboros was on its way to New Jersey and then into delis, drugstores, convenience stores, hotel lobbies, and markets all over the five boroughs.

The driver geared up and took the truck down the long lane lined by a mile of stacked Conex boxes rising either side of the road like steel Matterhorns.

He was out on a surface road heading for the on-ramp that would take him to I-4 and then I-75 for the two-day straight haul north.

A Range Rover pulled out from the lot of a derelict Tire Kingdom and fell into the truck's slipstream. The truck driver, bouncing to the Garifunka coming from his radio, never saw the SUV following at a discreet distance. Not even when the Rover followed him into a rest stop north of Wesley Chapel.

Hours later, county deputies and state troopers responded to calls about an explosion and fire out at the end of an unpaved road above Dade City. A truck and Conex container sat in a sandy area far from any houses, yet the blast was heard and felt for miles around. The whole mess was burning now, sending a thick pall of white smoke into the sky.

The cops sniffed the air. The smokers among them recognized the smell. Even the committed ex-smokers felt the old cravings returning.

The registered driver was found duct taped to a toilet in a stall at a rest stop down on I-75. The two staties who took his statement understood enough of his frantic Spanish to understand that he didn't see anything. Isaac "You've got to be fucking kidding me" Birnbaum swore that he was taking a piss at the urinals and that's the last thing he remembered before he came to bound and gagged on the cold porcelain of the *excusado*.

51

Gunny Leffertz said:

"Do the combat math. How do you subtract the maximum number of bad guys and still end the equation with your ass left over."

Symon Kharchenko received another FedEx box with another cell phone inside. No note this time.

"Yeah." The voice on the other end answered — the same man.

"All you are doing is digging a deeper grave for yourself," Symon said. He bit off every word.

"You have to ask yourself how much Dimi Kolisnyk is worth to you. My guess is that he's already cost you too much."

"You are a dead man."

"Give me the girl. Or give me Dimi."

"You think you will walk away from this?"

"Will you?"

The call ended.

Symon gripped the phone in his fist until the blood drained from his hand. He then set the phone down on the kitchen table.

His own phone rang. He keyed the cordless to talk. It was Yuri.

"We must meet. Now." Yuri was speaking between clenched teeth.

Yuri disconnected.

The meeting was in a private dining room at the back of a diner near the Clearwater causeway. Around the table there were only old men this time. Soshi, Yuri and Oreske were already there when Symon arrived. There was a chair for Wolo. A glass of vodka sat at the empty place.

They dispensed with the usual etiquette and niceties.

"How will you pay me?" Yuri demanded, a fisted hand on the table.

"I will buy you a new truck." Symon shrugged.

"Fuck the truck! I am down $15 million! Where is that? Where is my money?"

"You will get it. You have my word," Symon said.

"Your word!" Yuri struck the tabletop. Vodka sloshed from the glass before Wolo's chair.

"Give this man what he wants," Oreske said, his voice like stones grinding together.

"I would give him what he wants. What then? He goes away? We will never find him again."

"Who gives a fuck?" Yuri said in English.

"He killed my sons!" Symon protested.

"Were your idiot sons worth fifteen million? Or your pawn shops? How much did he take from you? How much more will he take from us?"

Symon's vision went white. He rose from his chair, palms flat on the tabletop.

Fat Soshi stood to press him back into the chair. The Georgian remained by him, a ham-sized hand on his shoulder. The man spoke slowly and deliberately, his voice resonant behind Symon.

"Call him, Symon. Give him the girl. Give him Dimi. The money is bad to lose. Worse is the police. They will connect these explosions and fires. They will not connect them to this Cade. They will connect them to us. This must end. It is what is best for all."

Symon nodded slowly. He picked up his own glass and drained it, eyes locked on Yuri across the table.

"Yes, this business with Levon Cade must end," Symon said to the table.

But our business is only beginning, Yuri Baghdasarian, he thought to himself.

52

Yvan pulled his BMW through the west entrance to the Florida State Fairgrounds just after dawn. Tupo sat by his side. They were following the directions relayed to them by Symon Kharchenko, directions the boss received from the American the night before.

They drove behind a long stable building to the place the American told them to park. A farm show had closed the day before. There were still wranglers here loading trucks with horses. The place smelled of animal shit and caramel corn. The rest of the park was a colorful, festive ghost town of fluttering banners and empty rides.

Tupo opened the back door of the BMW and pulled Dimi out by the arm. Dimi looked like a child in oversized sweats that still had the price sticker on them. Yvan bought them at Walmart to replace the clothes they'd cut off of their prisoner. Tupo gripped Dimi's elbow and guided him after Yvan who was walking away from the barn buildings toward the towering amusements at the other end of the grounds.

The walk toward their designated rendezvous took

them far from the car. Tupo was nearly carrying Dimi by the time they reached a row of benches that sat at the foot of a sloping water slide. Yvan studied the area for any sign of the American. There was nothing here but a shuttered beer garden standing against the rear of a large exhibition hall. The only other structure in sight was a Holiday Inn the other side of Martin Luther King, easily a half kilometer away.

Tupo sat Dimi down on the bench third from the left as directed. The big man stooped to run a hand under the bench and found a plastic bag attached with duct tape. The bag held a cell phone. Tupo tapped the send button twice.

53

Gunny Leffertz said:

"Where angels fear to tread. Ever hear that before? Ever hear about a place where even the angels won't go? Well, you're going to live there, pogie."

Through the 30x scope, the image of the trio approaching the benches before the water slide looked like a movie. Distance flattened the image to two dimensions.

On the roof of the Holiday Inn, Levon Cade lay prone atop an air conditioner housing. He swung the Model 70 slightly to the right to focus on the target bench. He looked up over the top of the rifle. The south parking lot of the fairgrounds and a long exhibition building lay between him and the foot of the slide. The lot was empty. Sparse early morning traffic drifted along this section of Martin Luther King. The rush and rumble of heavier traffic reached him from the raised length of I-4 audible through the trees behind him.

Dimi was lowered onto a bench by a guy built like a wrestler. The other guy, who looked like a Mongol warrior disguised in a designer running suit, stood scanning the surroundings with a professional eye. The man's hard eyes met Levon's through the scope.

The big man came up with the plastic bag that Levon planted there the night before. The cell in the pocket of his windbreaker shivered. Levon touched the button on his earpiece with a gloved finger.

"Yeah."

"We are here. What do you want us to do?"

"No girl."

"No girl. We have Dimi. What do you want us to do now?"

"Give Dimi the phone and walk away."

"That is all?"

"Give him the phone. Walk away. *Dosvedanya*."

Levon watched the big man take Dimi's hand and place the phone in it. The two men walked back the way they had come, leaving their prisoner seated on the bench. Dimi raised the phone to his ear.

"Hello?"

"Jenna Wiley."

"Was that her name?"

"Where is she?"

"That is what this is? I don't have her. I fucked her and left her."

"Left her where?"

"I don't have to tell you shit."

Levon squeezed the trigger of the rifle. The suppressor on the barrel lowered the big bore gun's report to a cough. The sound was lost in the buzz of traffic below.

Dimi leapt when the bench shuddered under him. Wood splinters sprayed over him. A fresh hole was drilled in the top board of the bench back to his right. The whole board, heavy redwood timber, was cracked end to end from the hole that appeared less than two feet away from him.

"Where is the girl?" the voice on the cell phone still clamped to his ear said.

"She's dead. I don't know what happened. I woke up and she was dead. Choked on puke."

"Because you drugged her."

"Shit. Sure. I guess."

"Where is she now?"

"I don't know. Buried somewhere. Dumped. I didn't ask. Shit."

"Someone took her then. Give me their name."

"Dutch. The biker you met at Cotton Lake. He took her off my hands. Did me a solid."

"Dutch Manklin."

"Yeah. You need to talk to him."

Through the scope, Levon trained the reticle at a point just above his target's head. Dimi was still speaking into the cell phone. Levon had cut the audio on his end to concentrate on the shot. Dimi was looking more and more agitated as he spoke, his eyes white in mute terror.

Levon brought pressure to the trigger. In the lens' eye, Dimi's head shifted out of view.

The bullet punched a hole in the bench back where Dimi had been a half second before.

Levon jacked in a fresh round while rising to a standing position. Far away the tiny figure of Dimi was running from the row of benches. Levon lifted the rifle and found Dimi in the scope as he was vaulting the ironing railing before the water slide area. He pressed the trigger, jacked a round, and found the target again. Dimi was hobbling at speed around the bottom edge of the water slide. Levon snapped a shot. His target kept moving until he was out of sight, the mass of the slide between them.

"Jesus Palomino," Levon said. He leapt from the air housing leaving the rifle behind. As evidence it was clean. He wore gloves while loading it. Any investigation into its background would reveal that it was on a list of ordnance believed destroyed in a copter crash in Herat in Afghanistan.

He wouldn't need the long-range rifle anymore.

Now was the time for working close.

54

Dimi screamed as loudly as his laboring lungs would allow him. He ran deeper into the grounds, crossing the lanes between the shacks, stalls, and more permanent buildings. Fear washed the pain from him. His body was wracked with deep aches from abuse at the hands of Yvan and Tupo. All of that was nothing compared to the startling agony rising from his calf.

The bullet caught him at the arc of his leap over the fence before the water slide. It ripped a furrow through the muscle at the back of his right calf. It was bleeding steadily. His whole leg went numb. Useless. He was dragging it now, feeling the pain begin to build as nerve endings got over their initial shock.

He called out as he shambled along a twisted path. There had to be someone here. Somebody had to hear him. It was the fucking state fair. The place was huge. There had to be someone still working here. Cleaners. Security. He'd call 911 himself but he'd left the cell phone behind when he bolted.

No one answered his cries. The grounds backed up

on surface streets. If he could reach one of them there would be cars and people. Someone would help him. He didn't care who. All he wanted was to get away from the maniac who was shooting at him. And Tupo and Yvan. He *really* wanted to get away from those two sick fuckers.

He stopped screaming then. The man after him and his former captors would hear him. They were probably already looking for him. There wasn't time for Tupo and Yvan to have made it back to their car. They wouldn't leave anyway. Not until they were sure it was over.

55

It wasn't over.

Levon was across Martin Luther King and into the ground's parking lot. He pulled the Rover as close as he could to a fair entrance. He jerked his gear bag from the back seat and leapt a turnstile to enter the grounds.

Between two exhibit halls, he stopped long enough to pull the Mariner from the bag. It was fully loaded with a plastic rack of five more twelve-gauge cartridges mounted on one side of the action. He grabbed a fistful of cartridges and stuffed them in a pocket of his windbreaker.

The cries from inside the park died away as he reached the benches before the water slide. He marked the direction of the shrieking voice. He found the splash of blood where his target jumped the railing. He was over it and following the spatters deeper into the amusement area. The target was taking a winding path, using cover. The blood trail was thinning; a collection of spots here and there as blood vessels collapsed around the wound.

The target was getting farther away as he followed the path of the waning blood trail that wound back and forth. He stopped tracking and headed on the straightest path for where he'd heard the last call for help. There was a bloody smeared handprint down the side of a corndog stand as he crossed the target's trail again. He stepped onto a broad midway and moved along one side at a trot, ears open for any sounds. The target was close. The target would break cover soon or hole up.

Levon didn't hear the first shots meant for him.

A jet flying low overhead on its climb out of Tampa International drowned out all sound with its passage. Concrete shards sprayed over the ground striking his legs. He turned, shotgun up. The larger of the two men who'd escorted Dimi into the park was running toward him between rows of seats set before a band shell. The man had an automatic raised in his fist, emptying it on Levon's position.

The second man, the Mongol warrior, was not in sight.

Levon dropped and rolled under the tarp of a concession stand. Rounds punched holes in the canvas. Glass from the canopy of a food warmer showered everywhere. Levon was out the back of the stand and moving low along a narrow alley that ran behind rows of stands. It was crowded with trash bins and stacked cartons. He was coming to the end of the lane when the second man stepped into view off a concourse.

Pumping round after round into the Mariner, Levon walked toward the man. Two loads of buck took the Mongol high in the chest, throwing him backwards. A third raked his legs as he fell. A fourth tore through the air, taking out the glass in front of a ticket kiosk. A nickel-plated handgun spun from the falling man's hand.

Levon stepped into the concourse and emptied the last round, a rifled slug, into the fallen man's head. The man's face vanished in a red mist. Levon slid over the counter of a concession stand. He lay on his back, reloading the Mariner, then settled down to listen.

A voice called in Russian, becoming more hushed as it approached. In the inch or so of clearance under the tarp covering the front of the counter, Levon could see a pair of feet approaching. They were in leather loafers, alligator maybe.

A hissed curse as the wrestler came into view of his fallen comrade. Levon held his breath and waited. The shadow of the man was visible through the sun-washed tarp.

Levon fired through the cloth. Three rounds of buck. He heard an agonized grunt as he rose to his feet. Levon trained the shotgun down on the big man lying in the dust of the concourse with his legs shot away. The man had fallen with his gun hand under him. He was struggling to roll and free it.

Another load of buck and a slug dropped him.

That left the prime target.

Levon reloaded as he walked.

56

Gunny Leffertz said:

"We all think of home until the day we have to come back and try to be the man we used to be. Then home can be the worst place on earth for us."

He caught up with Dimi Kolisnyk at the back of the grounds.

A parking area under sheltering oaks rose from the medians that separated the lanes.

The target made it to a high fence separating the fair from a residential neighborhood. He was hobbling along the fence line trying to find a way through, dragging the wounded leg behind him.

He never heard Levon coming through the trees toward him.

A round of buck swept his legs from under him.

He lay whimpering, raising bloody hands to Levon.

His mouth opened and closed soundlessly but for a whistling whine from deep in his throat.

The next load was center mass.

It lifted him from the ground in a cloud of dust.

His body was thrown against the fence.

The next stilled his convulsions.

His hands fell to the ground.

Levon dropped the shotgun where he stood. He stripped off the bloody windbreaker as he walked back into the fairgrounds. He shoved it down in a dumpster and walked on. The flannel shirt he wore underneath was a black and red check that hid the blood soaking into it.

There were no sirens until he reached the Range Rover. By itself, gunfire alone, even inside the city limits, was not a cause for immediate police response in Florida. He hooked a left off the lot and passed a pair of Tampa police cars whirling lights as he drove to the on-ramp for I-4 East.

He didn't stop until he saw the first signs for Disneyworld. That meant traffic and delays ahead. He pulled off and passed a few fast-food joints and convenience stores until he found a gas station with an exterior men's room. He washed the blood from his hands and face in the sink and changed from his flannel shirt into a hoodie from a Kohl's bag. He took the flannel shirt with him in the bag.

Levon ate breakfast at a Waffle House where he was advised that the Disney traffic usually died down a little after eleven. He grabbed a coffee to go and waited in the Range Rover until the eastbound lanes lightened up.

At long range parking at Orlando International, he took the Florida plates from a car without a layer of dust on it. He waited until he was past the city of Orlando and had hooked back west toward Apopka before switching the plates.

He listened to a news and talk station on the radio the whole way. No mention of a triple homicide in Tampa. Three dead white guys weren't worthy of breaking news these days.

It was evening by the time he turned the Rover onto 10 West for Huntsville.

57

Joe Bob Wiley looked twenty years older than the last time Levon had seen him. The man sat on the edge of the great room sofa he'd been sleeping on. Slept in his clothes for days maybe. The house smelled of fried food and stale beer.

"Wife left me. I told her to, but I think she wanted to go. She won't be back now, that's for sure," he said, rubbing the bristles on his face.

"You understand, this is the kind of news I had to tell you face to face," Levon said.

"I know. I know that. Thank you."

The men listened to the sounds of geese flying over the house for the lake. Joe Bob sat forward studying the carpet. Levon sipped the beer that the boss had insisted he help himself to.

"Is there any chance?" Joe Bob looked up, eyes red and tired.

Levon shook his head.

"Can't even have a funeral," Joe Bob said.

"I'd give that time. The police are still putting it all

together."

They listened to the quiet a while. Levon set down the half-empty bottle on a counter and stepped away from it.

"I owe you some money," Joe Bob said standing.

"No, you don't. I didn't deliver."

"To hell with that. I pay my bills."

Joe Bob left the room and came back with a check-book, one of those big corporate books. He leaned on the counter and wrote it out in a shaking hand. Levon stood watching him tear the check from the book ever so carefully. He handed the check to Levon. Fifty thousand.

"Shit, you had expenses, right?" Joe Bob said. He tried to tug the check from Levon's hand. Levon yanked it back, folded it, stuck it in his shirt pocket.

"I covered them. Consider this my severance. We're even."

"You're not coming back to work for me?" Joe Bob said. He looked relieved when Levon shook his head.

"I can't stay here. I kicked something over down there. They won't let it rest."

"What about me? They said they'd come back."

"That's just talk. They have their own problems. You can even put that away," Levon said. He nodded toward the shotgun leaning on the sofa.

"Well, okay then," Joe Bob said. His right hand fluttered at his side. Levon did not extend his own.

Levon walked alone to the Range Rover past the empty dog run. He drove for the interstate and Mississippi.

He stopped twice for gas and once for Wendy's drive-through. He got off the highway in Florence to pull up to a Walmart just long enough to stuff the endorsed check from Joe Bob into a Salvation Army pot.

58

An anonymous call led Florida state police to Trevor Lee Manklin (AKA' Dutch') and Douglas Raymond Ziemba (AKA 'Dougie') who were both in traction at Haley Veterans. Manklin suffered from multiple fractures to his legs and a split pelvic bone. Ziemba had several crushed vertebrae and broken ribs.

Blame the sweet, sweet painkillers or just being too damned tired and pissed off, the two bikers cooperated.

The next day cadaver dogs discovered the body of a Caucasian female aged eighteen to twenty-five in a grave dug for her in the scrub pines around Cotton Lake. She was packed in quicklime to hide her scent. No coyotes had dug her up.

She was tentatively identified as Jenna Marie Wiley. Her father flew down to Tampa to confirm it. Cause of death, as determined by the District Six medical examiner, was asphyxiation from the victim aerating vomitus into her lungs. Toxicity reports came back indicating high doses of Rohypnol in her blood. She was probably conscious as she died but with motor functions reduced to the point where she could not help herself. She just lay there and drowned. These details were not shared with the girl's father who didn't appear to have full control of motor functions himself.

State CID found enough DNA evidence at the home of one Dean Collins to establish it as the place where the Wiley girl died. Collins was three drawers down from Wiley in the cold room at the Hillsborough County morgue. His death was under investigation but appeared to be a part of some kind of gangland retribution. Two John Does lay in drawers near him; both found dead on the State Fairgrounds by Tampa cops responding to a "shots fired" call. A third shooter was being sought.

The two broken bikers had rock solid alibis.

It was a month later when a bolt action rifle with scope mounted atop it was found on the roof of a Holiday Inn off I-4. Two window-washers, Haitian illegals, discovered it when they were rigging their cage platform to one of the gantries along the roof line. They argued over what to do with it until one accepted forty bucks from the other for the right to keep it. The Model 70, rusted from exposure to heavy winter rains, was stuck in the back of a closet and forgotten after Patrice Saint-Felix's wife refused to let him hang it on their bedroom wall.

Barely mentioned in Tampa newspapers and websites was the apparent suicide of a local area businessman. Simon Kharchenko was apparently despondent over the recent death of his sons in a tragic single car accident near Ybor.

59

Gunny Leffertz said:

"What goes around, comes around. Bet your ass on that."

Spring comes slowly to upstate Maine. Snow lays in hollows in the woods until late May most years. The low sunlight takes its time reaching back into the piney deeps. The winds at night make one think that summer is a hope as far away as heaven.

In the warm confines of William King Elementary, it was career day. It was a small school with less than a hundred students and many of them siblings. Mom or dad or both were invited in to explain what they did for a living and answer questions from the kids. Doctors, veterinarians, car mechanics, truck drivers, skid operators, store owners, and web entrepreneurs were joining the classes, giving talks or demonstrations the whole day long.

Mrs. Balfour was concerned for Mary Tallmadge, a new student who'd arrived mid-year to join her fifth-grade class. She was the only student whose parent had not shown up today.

The little girl was by herself taking some cookies from the refreshment table set up in the gym.

"Is anyone coming from your house to give us a talk? Your mommy or daddy?" Mrs. Balfour asked.

"My mom's dead," Mary said. She did not turn from making her careful selections from the heaped cookie trays.

"I'm sorry." Mrs. Balfour blanched behind her smile. Damn it; she should have remembered that. Where was her head this morning?

"It's okay," Mary said and plucked a sugar cookie with rainbow sprinkles from atop a stack.

"What about your father? Didn't he want to come in and tell us all about his work?"

"He's retired."

"Well, he could come into the class and tell us about the work he retired from. What did your daddy used to do?"

"Do you really need to know that?" Mary said casually, without malice or discourtesy.

"I suppose not," Mrs. Balfour said, taken aback by the little girl's level gaze. She was relieved to see the principal gesturing her over to speak to a clutch of parents on the other side of the gym.

60

Dr. Jordan Roth, former master neurosurgeon of Huntsville, Alabama, was now Dr. Julian Hernandez running a pill mill in Plantation, Florida.

His identity, license and practice were all legitimate on paper. By all appearances, he ran a clinic at the back end of a professional park that had seen better days. The park contained weight loss places and cosmetic dentists for the most part. His new practice catered to Hispanics, mostly Cuban. It was all bilingual and the doctor had become quite fluent himself.

But Cubans do not like to visit doctors and resist taking any drugs prescribed to them. Consequently, Cubans tend to live longer.

The doctor's main clientele were shills sent to him with complaints of constant aches and chronic pains that required Schedule Three narcotics for relief. Jordan no longer exercised the invisible organ of his mind these days. Only his writing hand saw any action. The talented hand that once probed and repaired diseased and damaged brains now wrote prescriptions for a parade of deadbeats. These human debris resold these legal drugs for money to be used for the purchase of cheaper street drugs.

The outfit that kept Dr. Roth in his practice bought these drugs back from his patients. The outfit, some Jamaicans out of Miami, then retailed the prescription grade drugs at many times their value to users who liked their dope pure.

Just as these primo drugs were sold on, so was Jordan sold by the two men who held him. The two Russians from Tampa, the brute and the pop star, exchanged Dr. Roth for a truckload of stolen laptops. The Jamaican posse set him up here in the clinic. They owned him now. And they did indeed own him in every sense of the word.

The doctor was suspect number one in the murder of Marcia Roth. The case was a head scratcher for the Alabama state CID who took over the case. Mrs. Roth was found dead in the basement of their torched home with gunshot wounds to the head. The home was set ablaze, they theorized, to hide evidence of the crime. Following that, her husband, a renowned surgeon and local celebrity among the Huntsville elite, had disappeared from the face of the earth.

A further mystery was the whereabouts of the doctor's granddaughter who had been living with them at the time of the murder and fire. The little girl's father had also disappeared but was cleared of the arson and murder charges. Levon Cade was seen on security video from a Wendy's drive-through in Muscle Shoals, an hour's drive west, at the time of Marcia Roth's death.

A pet theory among the detectives was that Cade abducted his daughter and took off for parts unknown. He and the Roths had been in a bitter custody battle for months. The educated guess was that Cade picked his kid up at school and headed west with her.

Extrapolating on that, maybe the good doctor lost his shit over his son-in-law's actions. The book on Roth was that he could be a real stiff prick if he didn't get his way. One OR nurse had summed it up. "Surgeons." Accompanied by an epic eye roll.

So, the doc and his wife got in a fight over it and the doc blew her brains out.

As a motive, it stunk up the place. It was all they had. The doctor had not touched their bank accounts or retirement portfolios. He didn't even take the family car. Just shot the missus, set the house on fire, and walked away into the ether. Maybe he wandered into the woods and blew his own brains out. Maybe some hunters or hikers would find his bones one fine day.

These theories were all nonsense, of course. But Jordan Roth could never prove that. Who would believe a crazy story about Russian hitmen who killed his wife but let him live? Certainly not a bunch of cops looking to hang a murder around the neck of a famous surgeon.

He really thought he'd sold himself into a life of criminal adventure with Karp and Nestor. It was only another chapter in his life — a dull one at that.

Now he wrote scrips four days a week and read mystery novels on the beach the rest of the days. He had a condo in Pompano and a girlfriend who was a waitress at the Ebb Tide. He drank more than he should. He was having frequent headaches. He didn't sleep nights. Not well anyway.

When he did sleep, he had a dream. It was of the weekend he drove Arlene to college for her freshman year. In the dream, he is driving along a scenic road lined with green under blue skies. Arlene is as young in the dream as she was on that day. But in the dream, she wears a stained print hospital gown as she had the last time he saw her alive. She looks out the window and does not speak.

He tries to talk to her, but she does not turn her head. He can never remember what he says to her, only that he feels increasingly frustrated. Finally, he is shouting at her. She turns from the window to look at him without expression, without recognition. Arlene opens her mouth as if to say something. She reaches out to turn up the volume on the radio.

The music fills the car and drowns out his pleas for her to forgive him.

She turns away and looks out the window at the trees and clouds going by.

TAKE A LOOK AT BOOK TWO:
LEVON'S NIGHT

Chuck Dixon delivers book two in the dark, action-filled series—Levon Cade.

A gang of vicious criminals make the world their hunting ground as they search for a cache of hundreds of millions in stolen currency. Their search brings them to a snowbound community in the dead of Maine's vicious winter.

They came one night to torture, rob and kill. But they picked the wrong night…Levon's Night.

"The action is fierce and never lets up."

AVAILABLE NOW

ABOUT THE AUTHOR

Born and raised in Philadelphia, Chuck Dixon worked a variety of jobs from driving an ice cream truck to working graveyard at a 7-11 before trying his hand as a writer. After a brief sojourn in children's books he turned to his childhood love of comic books. In his thirty years as a writer for Marvel, DC Comics and other publishers, Chuck built a reputation as a prolific and versatile freelancer working on a wide variety titles and genres from Conan the Barbarian to SpongeBob Square-Pants. His graphic novel adaptation of J.R.R. Tolkien's *The Hobbit* continues to be an international bestseller translated into fifty languages. He is the co-creator (with Graham Nolan) of the Batman villain Bane, the first enduring member added to the Dark Knight's rogue's gallery in forty years. He was also one of the seminal writers responsible for the continuing popularity of Marvel Comics' The Punisher.

After making his name in comics, Chuck moved to prose in 2011 and has since written over twenty novels, mostly in the action-thriller genre with a few side-trips to horror, hardboiled noir and western. The transition from the comics form to prose has been a life-altering event for him. As Chuck says, *"writing a comic is like getting on a roller coaster while writing a novel is more like a long car trip with a bunch of people you'll learn to hate."* His Levon Cade novels are currently in production as a television series from Sylvester Stallone's Balboa Productions. He currently lives in central Florida and, no, he does not miss the snow.

Printed in Great Britain
by Amazon

41919845R00118